"I've just survived the longest night of my life,"

Ben said, "and I need some advice."

"So Candy 'Insomniac' Oakes kept you awake again?"

He hooted with laughter. "Yeah. I didn't get a wink of sleep."

I should look so wonderful after a sleepless night, Jenny thought. "Did Candy eat or drink anything with sugar in it before she went to bed?" she finally asked.

"Some ice cream," he told her. "And a soft drink."

"Skip those tonight," she advised, trying to keep her tone professional and her eyes off the back pockets of his jeans.

"Thanks, Jenny," he said, moving to the door. But instead of exiting, he suddenly strode to her side, hauled her into his open arms and kissed her thoroughly.

"Why'd you do that?" she whispered minutes later.

"Because your kisses are as sweet as candy," he said as he reached for her again, "and I've got a bad craving...."

Dear Reader,

It's March—and spring is just around the corner. We all know spring is the season of love, but at Silhouette Romance, every season is romantic, and every month we offer six heartwarming stories that capture the laughter, the tears, the sheer joy of falling in love. This month is no exception!

Honey, I'm Home by Rena McKay is a delightful reminder that even the most dashing hero is a little boy at heart, and Lindsay Longford's *Pete's Dragon* will reaffirm your belief in the healing power of love...and make-believe. The intense passion of Suzanne Carey's *Navajo Wedding* will keep you spellbound, the sizzling *Two To Tango* by Kristina Logan will quite simply make you want to dance, and Linda Varner's *As Sweet as Candy* will utterly charm you.

No month is complete without our special WRITTEN IN THE STARS selection. This month we have the exciting, challenging Pisces man in Anne Peters's *Storky Jones Is Back in Town.*

Throughout the year we'll be publishing stories of love by all your favorite Silhouette Romance authors—Diana Palmer, Suzanne Carey, Annette Broadrick, Brittany Young and many, many more. The Silhouette Romance authors and editors love to hear from readers, and we'd love to hear from *you!*

Happy Reading!

Valerie Susan Hayward
Senior Editor

LINDA VARNER

As Sweet as Candy

Published by Silhouette Books New York

America's Publisher of Contemporary Romance

If you purchased this book without a cover you should be aware that this book is stolen property. It was reported as "unsold and destroyed" to the publisher, and neither the author nor the publisher has received any payment for this "stripped book."

To Maureen Walters.
Thank you. Thank you. Thank you.

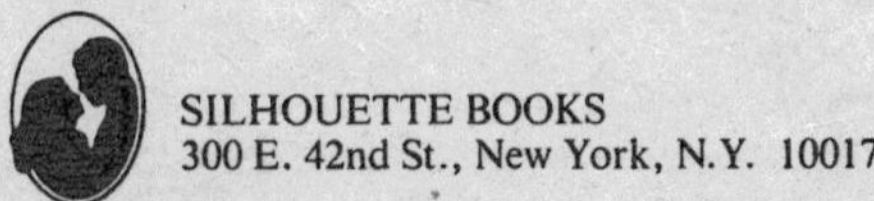

SILHOUETTE BOOKS
300 E. 42nd St., New York, N.Y. 10017

AS SWEET AS CANDY

Copyright © 1992 by Linda Varner Palmer

All rights reserved. Except for use in any review, the reproduction or utilization of this work in whole or in part in any form by any electronic, mechanical or other means, now known or hereafter invented, including xerography, photocopying and recording, or in any information storage or retrieval system, is forbidden without the permission of the publisher, Silhouette Books, 300 E. 42nd St., New York, N.Y. 10017

ISBN: 0-373-08851-5

First Silhouette Books printing March 1992

All the characters in this book have no existence outside the imagination of the author and have no relation whatsoever to anyone bearing the same name or names. They are not even distantly inspired by any individual known or unknown to the author, and all incidents are pure invention.

®: Trademark used under license and registered in the United States Patent and Trademark Office and in other countries.

Printed in the U.S.A.

Books by Linda Varner

Silhouette Romance

Heart of the Matter #625
Heart Rustler #644
Luck of the Irish #665
Honeymoon Hideaway #698
Better to Have Loved #734
A House Becomes a Home #780
Mistletoe and Miracles #835
As Sweet as Candy #851

LINDA VARNER

has always had a vivid imagination. For that reason, while most people counted sheep to get to sleep, she made up romances. The search for a happy ending sometimes took more than one night, and when one story grew to mammoth proportions, Linda decided to write it down. The result was her first romance novel.

Happily married to her junior high school sweetheart, the mother of two and a full-time secretary, Linda still finds that the best time to plot her latest project is late at night when the house is quiet and she can create without interruption. Linda lives in Conway, Arkansas, where she was raised, and believes the support of her family, friends and writers' group made her dream to be published come true.

MUSTS IN A MATE

A wifely checklist*
custom designed
for
Benjamin Carlton Ryder

1. Must have long brown hair.
2. Must have big brown eyes.
3. Must be petite.
4. Must be a good cook.
5. Must love kids.
6. Must be a good housekeeper.
7. Must love animals.
8. Must be a good money manager.
9. Must be good in bed.

*Not necessarily in order of importance

Chapter One

"I'm sorry. You simply cannot have this baby without some form of ID."

The manager of Kidstuff Day-care Center, who'd just introduced herself as Jennifer Robbin, smiled sweetly when she said those words, but Ben Ryder could tell that she meant every one of them.

He snorted his impatience. "Give me a break! Not only did you get a telephone call from Mrs. Pruitt informing you that I was coming for Candy, you've found my name on a permission slip in her file. What more could you possibly want?"

"Some form of ID," she repeated again, clearly undaunted by his bad temper.

Swallowing his retort, Ben rechecked the pockets of his mud-splattered jeans. He knew the search was futile, however. His wallet was at home, probably lying on the table right next to where his keys had been when he'd gotten that frantic phone call from his niece's baby-sitter.

"Look," he said. "I understand your concern, I appreciate your caution, and I'd love to cooperate—*if* I had my wallet with me. Unfortunately, it's at home."

"Then why don't you go get it?" Ms. Robbin suggested quite calmly.

"Because there isn't time!" Ben exploded. "I live clear out of town on a nearly impassable road, and you close—" he glanced at his watch "—make that *closed* at six o'clock. I've already kept you ten minutes late as it is."

"That's perfectly all right," she replied. "I'll be glad to wait here with Candice until you get back." The obstinate set of her pretty little chin told Ben she would do battle before she'd change her mind. Having been raised with four sisters who were every bit as stubborn as this woman appeared to be, Ben knew when to give up. He turned on his heel and stalked toward the exit without another word, managing to make it halfway across the reception area before he heard a familiar cry.

"Nuh-Ben! Nuh-Ben!"

With a grin of delight, Ben whirled toward that magical sound to discover that Candy had toddled into the room, all smiles and heading in his direction. He flicked a look of triumph at Ms. Robbin, who would not meet his gaze, then started toward his niece, only to halt abruptly when the manager intercepted the child, scooping her up.

"First, the ID," she stated, actually adding an apologetic shrug.

"But Candy obviously knows me," Ben argued.

"She knows Oscar the Grouch, too, but that doesn't mean I'd let her go home with him."

Oscar the Grouch? Ben nearly choked. "You're being unreasonable."

"I'm being careful. Rules are rules. As much as I'd like to, I simply cannot break them. Surely you can understand that."

In all honesty, Ben could, and abruptly he sighed his defeat. "I'll be back within the hour," he promised curtly, pivoting to stride from the room. Muttering to himself about sisters on cruises and unreliable baby-sitters, Ben quickly exited the building and walked to his truck.

He noted that the rainstorms of the past three days, so typical of September, had momentarily ceased. Maybe that swamp—jokingly referred to as a road—on which he lived would soon dry out. Meanwhile, he would have to negotiate it at least three more times this day, damn the luck.

Face grim, Ben climbed into his vehicle and inserted the key—or tried to. In his agitation, he missed the ignition altogether and dropped the ring, which hit the floor with a jingle. He bent down automatically to pick it up, freezing when his gaze fell on the stack of mail he'd retrieved from the post office the day before and had never gotten around to reading.

With a grunt of satisfaction, he snatched up the September issue of *Equine* and fumbled through it for the article he'd written on the art of shoeing horses. There was a photograph of him demonstrating the craft—a photo anyone should consider positive ID...even bullheaded day-care managers.

Bullheaded? Because she wouldn't hand Candy over to a man who called himself her uncle, but had no proof of identification? Ben shook his head, suddenly remorseful about his actions over the past few minutes. Clearly he owed Ms. Robbin an apology. She'd been nothing but polite, if firm, and he had no explanation for his temper except his anxiousness to begin this unexpected week with his niece, who was as sweet as her name and fun with a capital *F*.

Magazine in hand, Ben maneuvered the puddled drive once more to walk back to the day-care with determined strides. There was no one in the reception area this time, but he heard voices coming from a room to his right and so he made tracks in that direction. There, he found a carpeted play area, dotted with child-sized tables and chairs, bookshelves and easels. At one of those tables sat Ms. Robbin and Candy, their backs to him, heads bent over a book. Since the chair was so low, the manager had tucked her long legs to one side, a position that widened the slit in her skirt and revealed a tantalizing length of shapely calf and thigh.

Connoisseur that he was, Ben stole a moment to take advantage of the view. His gaze moved upward naturally, noting the rest of her apparel—a matching jacket with padded shoulders and a contrasting scarf—before settling on her mass of hair. Dark brown and curly, it contradicted the sternness of the business suit by cascading halfway down her back. Ben found his fingers were itching to see if it was really as soft as it looked.

Startled and maybe a bit flustered by the intensity of his desire to touch, Ben came to life and cleared his throat with deliberate loudness. Ms. Robbin turned, blinked her surprise and swiftly stood, knocking over the chair in her haste.

"I—I didn't expect you back so soon," she stammered, smoothing down her skirt, straightening her jacket. "You have the ID already?" Ben noticed that her cheeks glowed pink, defining the delicate bone structure of her face, accentuating the cherry red of her full lips. Her dark brown eyes—thickly lashed and almond-shaped—were wide with surprise now, giving her an exotic look Ben would have found irresistible another place, another time. Right now he couldn't afford such foolishness. Jennifer Robbin was a very definite obstacle to a much-desired week with his niece.

"I've got something that should suffice," he said, crossing the room to join them.

Jenny noted that his handsome face was as flushed as hers felt. Clearly he was not pleased with the way things had gone thus far, and she regretted that fact. But as she'd told him earlier, rules *were* rules. Candice Oakes had been a regular at Kidstuff since the age of six months, when her mother, Donna, got her secretarial job. Candy was a favorite around the day-care, and not for anything would Jenny let a virtual stranger waltz in and take her home—not even this one, with his plausible story, trustworthy face and ebony eyes so like his sister's.

Jenny remembered the glow of excitement in Donna's eyes that very Friday morning when she and her husband, Andy, dropped their daughter off at the day-care on their way to the plane to begin their week-long vacation. It was a shame that the baby-sitter's elderly mother had suddenly taken ill way off in Texas and darned lucky that Donna had a brother willing to donate his weekends and nights to the cause.

Brother? Undoubtedly, she admitted. The family resemblance was remarkable. Unfortunately, more than that was required before Jenny could release one of her charges to a stranger, and, on that thought, she put out a hand for the credit card or driver's license he must have found in his vehicle. But Ben handed her a magazine instead.

"What's this?" Jenny asked, staring in bewilderment at the glossy cover which sported a full-color photo of a horse.

"My ID," Ben answered. "Turn to page sixty-five. You'll find an article I wrote. There's a picture of me at the end of it."

Jenny did as requested, gazing for long moments at the photo in question. It was Ben Ryder, all right, standing in front of what appeared to be a barn or shed. Dressed in a pair of snug-fitting jeans, and a western-styled shirt with a red bandana knotted at the neck, he looked as though he'd stepped back in time. The hammer and tongs he wielded merely enhanced the tantalizing image, as did the fire, the anvil and the red-hot horseshoe he held suspended before him.

There was no mistaking his identity, especially in light of the caption under the picture: *Dr. Ben Ryder Demonstrating His Skill At Rowdy River.*

"You can see that it's me," Ben said.

"Yes," she agreed, reluctantly dragging her gaze from the picture to the marvelously male specimen before her.

"And you're satisfied?"

"Yes. . . ."

He smiled his triumph—a gypsy-white smile that she felt clear to the bone. Baffled by her suddenly racing pulse and the butterflies in her stomach, Jenny closed the magazine and thrust it at him.

"You're a blacksmith?"

"Only for show." He folded the magazine over so he could stick one end of it in his back pocket. "I actually make my living as a veterinarian." At that, Ben stepped past Jenny to approach his niece and drop to one knee beside the child. "Hey, kiddo."

"Nuh-Ben," she said, smiling and reaching out for him.

"Nubbin?" Jenny questioned in disbelief. The man stood six foot two if he stood an inch.

Ben picked up the mop-headed youngster and kissed her soundly before meeting Jenny's curious gaze. "Nuh-Ben," he corrected solemnly. "Eighteen-month-old for Uncle Ben."

"Oh." Jenny felt her face get hot again. Since Ben was already halfway to the door, she had to run to catch up with him. "Wait. You forgot Candy's bag."

"What bag?"

"Her diaper bag. It should have extra diapers, a change or two of clothes, another pair of shoes...." Jenny frowned, suddenly suspicious. "Do you have any children of your own, Dr. Ryder?"

"I'm not married."

"I...see. Um, have you ever kept your niece before?"

"Lots of times."

"Overnight?"

"Well, no, but how hard can it be?"

He had to be kidding. The butterflies in Jenny's stomach suddenly took flight, this time for another reason altogether. Clearly the man was a novice at baby-sitting and had no idea what lay in store for him. Somehow, and with tact, she would have to clue him in. "Children at this age are very active, Dr.—"

"Call me Ben."

She nodded, swallowed hard, and tried again. "Candy is a very busy little girl. You won't be able to leave her for a minute."

"I realize that," he retorted, obviously insulted in spite of Jenny's careful choice of words.

Though dismayed by this development, Jenny felt that she had no option but to proceed. "Forgive me for prying, but is your house child-proofed?"

"Yes," Ben said. "Donna took care of that one Sunday when they came out for a barbecue."

"Good. Do you have any pets?"

"A dog . . ."

Uh-oh.

"And a cat . . ."

Double trouble.

"Indoors. Outside, I have rabbits, some ducks, a few squirrels. . . ."

Oh, Lord. "Then may I suggest that you lock them all up while you have your niece."

"But they wouldn't hurt a fly," Ben argued. "Much less Candy."

"It's not Candy I'm worried about," Jenny said. "Now what groceries do you have in the house?"

"What difference does that make?" he asked. "She has teeth."

"And a notoriously delicate stomach."

"I'm a doctor, for God's sake," Ben exploded. "I know what babies eat."

"And speaking of which, don't doctors often get emergency calls? What are you going to do if you get one?"

"Another vet and I swap weekend calls. It's his weekend."

"What about next week? You'll have her from 6:00 p.m. to 6:00 a.m. Monday through Friday. What will you do if someone phones at midnight needing help?"

"I'm not an obstetrician," Ben said. "I don't get that many night calls."

"But what if you get one next week?" Jenny persisted.

"I'll cross that bridge when I get to it, okay?" He sighed. "You sound just like Donna, for Pete's sake. I volunteered to keep Candy when she first told me about this cruise. Would you believe she *laughed* at me?"

Jenny certainly would.

"She said flat-out she didn't need my help. Said she'd lined up a very reliable sitter who would keep Candy this weekend and then take her to the day-care all next week." He shook his head. "Some reliable sitter. That woman actually thought I'd be *pleased* that she'd arranged for some cousin or other to fill in for her. I told her there was no way I was going to leave Candy with strangers."

"Does this cousin have children?"

Ben frowned. "Why do you ask?"

"I just thought—"

"I know exactly what you thought," he retorted. "And you can think again. I'm her uncle. She goes home with me. Now would you just get the bag?"

Jenny got it.

"Thank you," Ben said when she thrust it at him. Somewhat softer, he added, "I really appreciate your concern, but I know what I'm doing," before he headed to the exit again.

Not nearly as certain of that as he was, Jenny hurried after them. "My landlady doesn't allow children in my apartment complex, but maybe if I—"

"You live in an apartment that doesn't allow kids?" Ben demanded incredulously, whirling to face her.

Jenny, who'd been right on his heels, ran smack into him. She gulped under his censorious look, took a step back and almost answered the question before she remembered that she didn't owe this man any explanation for her choice of residence. "Yes, I do, but maybe if I begged, she would let me keep Candy at my place just this one week."

"And why should you do that?" Ben asked, just as Candy reached out to grasp a double handful of Jenny's curls in her fat little fist and yanked—hard.

"That's...oww...why," Jenny gasped, blinking back tears. "Candy's unpredictable."

"Holy moly!" Ben exclaimed, tugging his niece's fingers loose. He captured her now-empty hands in his and held them out of harm's way. "Sorry about that, but your hair *is* beautiful. I'm tempted to grab a handful myself. Now don't worry. I assure you I can handle anything...even Candy."

Sensing that he wasn't going to be swayed, Jenny gave in as graciously as possible and dug one of her business cards out of her jacket pocket. "At least take my card. My home number is on it and I won't mind a bit if you call for help. I don't have any big plans for the weekend."

"You don't?"

"Well, nothing I couldn't cancel if I needed to," she amended, wishing she hadn't been quite so honest. He might assume she stayed home out of necessity and not by choice. Why that bothered her, she had no idea. Jenny was proud of her independence.

"You won't need to," he assured her briskly, stepping through the door, striding toward the muddiest truck Jenny had ever seen.

"Do you have a car seat?" she yelled after him.

Ben halted, shoulders suddenly sagging. Slowly he turned back to face her, a look of utter disgust on his face. "I forgot all about that."

"I'll loan you one," Jenny offered hastily, sensing he was near the end of his tether. In minutes Ben had secured the seat in the truck and strapped a protesting Candy into it.

"That ought to do it," he said, turning to face Jenny again. "May I keep it until next weekend?"

She nodded.

He gave her one of those breathtaking smiles. "Thanks. We'll be leaving now, Ms. Robbin. I've got a lot of stops before I head for home." He paused, scanning her worried expression, then added, "If it'll make you feel any better about this whole thing, I swear I'll phone if I get in a jam."

"Please do, and call me Jenny," she said, warily eyeing the precocious child who'd just unfastened her seat belt and now reached for the radio knobs with both hands. Under her breath, she added, "Something tells me we're going to be old friends before I get my car seat back."

"What are you doing?" Jenny asked her best friend, Krissie Hart, an hour later when the bubbly blonde drove into the parking lot of Sports Emporium, Springfield, Missouri's world-famous sporting-goods store.

"Parking the truck," Krissie replied, maneuvering the vehicle between the yellow stripes painted on the asphalt and killing the engine with a flick of the key.

Jenny frowned. "Here?"

"Here." Krissie tossed her ponytail back over her shoulder and dropped her key ring into her purse. She opened the door and jumped to the pavement, then turned to look back at Jenny, who hadn't budged from where she sat next to her. "Move it, woman. You've got places to go, men to meet, things to do—" she chuckled wickedly "—I hope."

Jenny wasn't amused. "In *there?*" She pointed to the brightly lit building, which was several blocks long.

"In there," Krissie replied firmly.

"You've got to be kidding."

Krissie huffed her impatience. "Would I kid about something as serious as spinsterhood? You'll be thirty years old in ten days. We've got to find a Mr. Perfect for you...and quick."

"Why? I do all right alone."

"Now you do. What about when you're old and gray?"

"Thirty is a far cry from old and gray," Jenny said, used to the familiar argument. Krissie, who'd been married for three whole months, thought everyone else should be, too. Sometimes it was darned annoying. "What kind of man do you think we're going to find in a sporting-goods store anyway?"

"An athlete."

Jenny groaned. "Just what I need in my life...an egocentric jock."

"Okay then, scratch the athlete idea. We'll look for a fisherman or, better yet, a hunter. There's not a woman alive who can resist the rugged, outdoors type."

A sudden vision of a handsome man in mud-caked jeans filled Jenny's head. Ruthlessly, she erased it. "Except me. Frankly, I could never be serious about a man with murder in his heart and Bambi in his rifle sights."

"Maybe if you tried a little harder, you could," Krissie retorted, throwing her hands up in exasperation.

"No, I couldn't. And what do I need with the outdoors type anyway? I'm a city girl, or will be, if that Kansas City director job I heard about pans out."

"That kind of job is not for you. Why, this managerial position is bad enough. As a director you would lose all contact with children, which is the very reason you became a child-care specialist in the first place."

"But I need a change, Krissie. A new job will definitely do the trick."

"So would a social life—the reason I'm trying to find you a man," Krissie argued. "Sometimes you're as baffling as my freshman English students, Jennifer Robbin, and that's going some. To think that I thought it would be a snap to discover what type of man appealed to you. So far you've nixed cultured, artistic and intelligent. If you don't give rugged a shot, I don't know what I'm going to do."

"Give up on me?" Jenny asked hopefully.

"Never," Krissie replied. "I'm going to find you a reason to stick around if it kills us both."

"As well it may. Why don't you just admit defeat? So far you've dragged me to the theater, an art exhibit and a lecture. Did we find one suitable man in any of those places?"

"No, we found hundreds of them. Unfortunately, not one appealed to you."

"Then what makes you think tonight will be any different?"

"My eternal optimism, that's what," the blonde replied. "And a firm belief that somewhere out there waits a sensitive, caring man who loves kids as much as you do. And once you lay eyes on him, you'll forget every doubt, every fear, and every crazy notion of moving to Kansas City. He's not only going to knock your socks off, Jennifer Robbin, he's going to blow your mind!"

"That's just what I'm afraid of," Jenny murmured, suddenly reminded of her mother. Once widowed, twice divorced, fifty-one year old Marilyn Montgomery was now dating a man five years younger. For this true love, she had dyed her hair and bought a sports car she couldn't afford—a sure sign she'd lost her head, heart and identity...again. It seemed as though Marilyn would never be her own woman or appreciate the importance of independence. Jenny, who had watched her parent sacrifice her all to the men in her life, had also witnessed the painful results. As a result, she had long since vowed she would never do the same.

Krissie reached out to pat Jenny's hand. "I know you believe that marriage is all give and no take—at least for the wife. And I understand why you feel that way. Lord knows, I would, too, if I had your poor mother as a role model. I just wish I could make you realize that all relationships are not as one-sided as hers have been."

"Oh? Name one that isn't."

Krissie smiled proudly. "Why, mine, of course."

"Ha!" Jenny responded. "Who moved in with whom when you and Jack got married?"

"You know I moved in with him."

"And I also know that you gave up the most gorgeous apartment in Springfield to do it."

"His was closer to the lumberyard."

"But farther from the university."

"I wanted to move in with him," Krissie stated flatly, crossing her arms over her chest.

Jenny, who suspected differently, ignored that. "Whose car got traded in when Jack decided he needed a truck?"

"Mine," Krissie said, "but only because we knew we'd get more money for it."

"Bull. That little red number of his would've gotten twice what your sedan did and you know it. He just didn't want to give it up and now he makes *you* drive the truck." Krissie's answering silence told Jenny she'd hit a raw nerve, and suddenly remorseful, she abandoned her argument. "I'm sorry. What you and Jack do is none of my business."

"And what you do is none of mine?" Krissie questioned with a heavy sigh.

"Exactly."

"I'm only doing this out of love. Love, and desperation. What will I do if you leave Springfield?"

"Miss me. And I'll miss you. We'll survive, though. And if everything goes according to plan, I'll be back in a few years with enough money and experience to open my own day-care center right here in Springfield."

"Your big dream?"

"My big dream."

Krissie gazed at her in silence for a moment, then laughed softly. "You're right, of course. You always are. I apologize for nagging. If you don't want to go into Sports Emporium, we'll go get pizza instead. First, though, I have to run inside and get a couple of boat cushions. Jack and I are going fishing Sunday—our last chance before the fall semester starts and I get tied up with my classes."

"I thought you hated fishing," Jenny responded in surprise.

"I do," Krissie said. "But Jack wanted to go, so I..." Her voice trailed off into silence and she shrugged sheepishly. "Oh, all right. I admit it. I probably do most of the compromising, but if I do, it's by choice. I'm crazy about that man."

"And no wonder," Jenny replied. "He can be such a sweetheart and is totally crazy about you, too. Unfortunately, he's also spoiled rotten, just like all the rest of the males in this man's world." She shook her head. "Men. Can't live with them, can't live without them."

"I don't believe it!" Krissie exclaimed with a gay laugh. "You actually admitted it."

"I do, on occasion, get lonesome for the opposite sex," Jenny reluctantly admitted. "And when I do, I simply recite the list of typical male characteristics that I put to memory years ago, when Mom got her first divorce. That invariably gets my head back on straight."

"Oh really? What, exactly, is on this list of yours?"

"Besides spoiled rotten, which I've already mentioned, there's selfish, manipulative, arrogant and preoccupied with sex."

"Yipes," Krissie murmured with a wince. "Sorry I asked." She gave Jenny a long speculative look. "Does this mean that you assume every man you meet has each characteristic on this list until he proves otherwise?"

"That's right," Jenny replied.

"But how can they if you won't give them a chance?"

Jenny grinned. "Darned if I know."

"No wonder you're still single," Krissie grumbled. "I sure wish there was something I could say to make you see how wrong you are."

"Trust me, there isn't," Jenny assured her. "Now would you please hurry up and get those boat cushions? I'm starved."

Krissie hesitated as though she wanted to say something else, then shrugged and turned away. As the blonde walked toward the building, Jenny rolled down the window to let in some fresh air. With a sigh she settled back in the seat and closed her eyes, lost in thoughts of marriages—happy and unhappy ones. As manager of all three of the Kidstuff Day-care Centers in Springfield, Jenny naturally saw both kinds on a daily basis. There were far more unhappy ones, in her opinion. And each of those, coupled with kaleidoscoped memories of every macho man who'd darkened her mother's door, reinforced Jenny's belief that solo was the only way to fly.

As she'd told Krissie moments before, it was strictly a man's world. And no wonder. Even in this day of so-called liberation, women still pandered to them. All but Jenny, that is. Quite content and comfortable with the woman she had become, she steadfastly refused to be counted in the numbers of females who sacrificed their all for the men they loved. And if Krissie devoted an eternity to her search for Jenny's Mr. Perfect—a man who would appreciate her for what she was and respect her right to a separate identity—Jenny knew she would never find him.

No such man existed.

"Holy moly!"

Jolted rudely from her thoughts, Jenny glanced out the window toward the sound of that suspiciously familiar outcry. Though he stood several yards away with his back to her, Jenny recognized not only Ben Ryder's wide shoulders but his mud-splashed 4×4, parked one vehicle away from the one in which she sat. She leaned forward, craning her neck for a better view of the man, who now peered through the glass on the passenger side of his truck, obviously agitated about something.

"Candy, honey, I've locked myself out. Can you reach the door handle?"

Oh my God. Jenny reached for her own, catching herself just in time. Ben had told her in no uncertain terms that he could handle his niece. Now was the perfect opportunity to find out if he really could.

"Atta girl!" she heard him exclaim. "Get a good grip on it and pull!"

But the door didn't open. Ben's shoulders slumped with his disappointment, and in spite of her sympathy for him, Jenny almost laughed. So he could handle anything, huh?

"Let's try again, okay? No, don't get out of the car seat. Don't... all right then, *do.* Now I want you to put your hand on the door handle. No, sweetie, not the radio, the door handle. That's right. No, no. Not the glove box, and *not* the stick shift. The door handle, Candy. *The door handle.*"

Jenny did laugh this time and then bit her lip to keep it in check. Poor man. And he had his mischievous niece not only for the weekend but every night for a whole week.

"Candy, no. No! Don't touch the sack. There are nasty ol' fishhooks in there. They'll bite you."

Fishhooks? Jenny's amusement vanished.

"That's right, sugar. Leave it alone. Now come over here and— *What have you got now?*"

Jenny held her breath.

"Holy moly, my keys! You found my keys. No, Candy, don't put them in your mouth. No, no. Not in the ignition, either. No. Candy, honey, no. Don't do it. *Aw, hell!*"

Chapter Two

Her heart in her throat, Jenny leapt from Krissie's truck and bounded to the rescue, unceremoniously pushing Ben aside.

"Candice!" she called, tapping on the glass. "Come over here and see Miss Jenny. Hurry now... quick as a bunny."

Candy's big brown eyes grew even bigger. She squealed her delight and abandoned the keys to scramble across her empty car seat to the window where Jenny and Ben hovered anxiously.

Jenny heard Ben's "Whew!" from behind her and whirled on him. "How could you do such an idiotic thing?"

"It was an accident. I had the key ring in my hand. Must have dropped the darned thing when I put Candy in the car seat."

"That's great, just great," Jenny muttered, all the while forcing herself to smile and wave at Candy to keep the child distracted. "Now what are you going to do?"

"Beats the heck out of me. The locks are designed to resist break-in and Candy's not strong enough to open the door."

Not strong enough? Candy Oakes, who could do one-armed chin-ups on a playpen? Jenny shook her head in disbelief and patted her jacket pockets in search of one of the sugar-free suckers she routinely stashed there. She sighed her relief when her fingers closed around the looped safety stick of one. In moments, Jenny had the bright red confection unwrapped and dangling before Candy.

"Look what I've got," she told Ben's adorable nemesis. "Want it?"

"Mine," Candy responded, reaching out. She slapped at the glass barrier with both hands, screeching her dismay.

"Open the door and I'll give it to you," Jenny said.

Candy opened the door.

"Well, I'll be damned," Ben murmured as Jenny reached inside for his niece.

"Watch your language," Jenny snapped. Flicking him a hard look, she handed the sucker to Candy. When the moppet had deposited the sweet into her mouth, Jenny lifted her out of the truck. Ben reached out, but Jenny shook her head, not quite willing to hand over her precious bundle. "Are you sure you're up to this? I'll be more than glad to call my landlady and—"

"I'm up to it."

"But you've still got the whole weekend to go, not to mention every night next week."

"I'm up to it, dammit!"

Jenny took one look at those glistening dark eyes of his and knew he truly believed what he said. Though tempted to press the point, she didn't. Ben Ryder was nothing to her, after all. She had no emotional stake in his success or failure except as far as Candy's welfare was concerned, and she knew in her heart of hearts that the child would be safe with her uncle.

"Watch your language," she therefore repeated as she acknowledged defeat and passed his niece to him.

Candy reached out her left arm for Ben, hooking it around his neck as he took her. Unfortunately, she didn't release her right-armed stranglehold of Jenny, who was obliged to take a stumbling step forward. Suddenly nose to nose with Ben, a very disconcerted Jenny had to tip her head back to avoid being mouth to mouth.

"Sugar," Candy said. "Nuh-Ben sugar."

"I think she wants you to kiss me," Ben said, so close that his words fanned Jenny's burning cheeks. Jenny heard the rumble of laughter in his voice, saw the twinkle in his eye.

"I think not," she retorted with embarrassing breathlessness. Ducking under Candy's arm, Jenny stepped back. Her heart hammered so loudly she feared Ben would hear it, but if he did, he didn't let on. Instead, he shrugged as though he couldn't care less that they'd disappointed his niece.

"Now that you have the situation in hand, I'd better be going," Jenny said with a calm she didn't feel. "Good luck."

"I assure you that I won't need it," Ben told her. "Everything has gone fine until now. We just finished watching the scuba diver feed the fish. Now we're going to get French fries and a chocolate sundae."

"Scuba diver?"

"In the tank inside Sports Emporium," he explained, reaching into his pocket to extract a snowy white handkerchief with which he dabbed Candy's sticky chin. "Surely you've seen it."

Jenny glanced toward the store and frowned. "Actually, I've never been in there."

"Then what are you doing here?" It was Ben's turn to frown. "You weren't checking up on me, were you?"

"Don't be silly, Dr. Ry—"

"Ben, remember?"

"I have better things to do than trail you. I'm here with a friend. I was waiting in that truck over there when I spotted you."

"Next time go inside with him. You'll love the tank. It's enormous and full of all kinds of freshwater fish. Candy and I come by every time we can."

"So there you are!"

Jenny turned at the sound of Krissie's voice. She found the blonde approaching with rapid steps, boat cushions clutched to her chest.

"I didn't see you at first," Krissie said. "Couldn't imagine where you'd gone." She looked directly at Ben and offered her hand. "I'm Krissie Hart."

"Ben Ryder," he said, shifting Candy to his other arm to free his right hand. "This is Candy."

"What a doll," Krissie said after the brief handshake. "She's got your eyes."

"Actually, she has my sister's eyes," Ben told her with a pleased grin. "This is my niece. She's staying with me for a while."

Krissie laughed at her mistake. "Do you have any children of your own?"

"I'm not married."

"Oh?" Krissie arched an eyebrow and glanced over to Jenny, who glared daggers at her and shook her head very slightly. With an impish grin, Krissie shifted her gaze back to Ben. "You must really love kids to take on one this size."

"I adore them. Especially this size."

Krissie's grin widened. "No kidding. So does Jenny. But if you've known her any time at all you already know that."

"Hadn't we better get going?" Jenny interjected, attempting to give her talkative, too-curious friend a firm nudge in the direction of the truck. "The pizza parlor gets really crowded around seven-thirty."

"Especially on Friday nights," Krissie agreed, neither budging nor switching her gaze from Ben. "Do you two have dinner plans? We'd love to have you join us."

"Krissie!" Jenny gasped. With difficulty, she managed a tight-lipped smile. "They're going to get French fries."

"And a sundae," Ben added solemnly, though his lips twitched with what could only be mirth.

Jenny was not amused. "Have a nice, uneventful weekend, Dr.—uh—Ben. I'll see you both Monday morning." With that, she pushed Krissie none-too-gently out of harm's way.

"Don't worry about a thing, Jenny Wren," Ben called after them. "I still have your phone number."

"Jenny *Wren?*" Krissie squeaked the moment they were out of sight.

"He meant Robbin, I'm sure. He just got the wrong bird."

"But the right phone number, I'll bet."

"Shut up, Krissie."

Krissie did—until they reached the truck. Then she laughed. "Sorry if I embarrassed you, but he was such a cutie and you were so obviously enthralled—"

"I was not enthralled!" With a huff of exasperation, Jenny scrambled into the vehicle, slamming the door behind her with a vengeance. By the time Krissie got in on the other side, Jenny had crossed her arms over her chest to sit in stony silence, her agitated breaths the only sound in the truck.

"You were, you know," Krissie said as she inserted the key into the ignition. "Why, I've never seen you this way before-bright-eyed, blushing. I'll bet your heart is racing a mile a minute." She reached out as though to take Jenny's pulse and got her hand slapped for her efforts.

"I was upset," Jenny said. "Still am." Quickly she recounted the events of that evening, beginning with Ben's arrival at the day-care.

"So he's a vet."

"That's right," Jenny replied with a couldn't-care-less shrug.

"Then relax. That proves he's reasonably intelligent, not to mention sensitive and caring." She gave Jenny a guileless look and started the engine. "Besides which, he obviously loves kids. You'd better latch on to him, *Jenny Wren.* He might be the one we've been looking for."

"Very funny."

"I'm serious. He's everything you want, plus stable, hardworking, established...."

"How on earth could you tell all that from a three-minute encounter?"

"Gut instinct," Krissie told her, adding, "which beats the heck out of that stupid list of yours."

"My list is not stupid," Jenny countered. "And as for Ben Ryder being 'the one'... well, you can just put that right out of your head. I'm never going to see the man again."

Ben tested the temperature of the scant inch of water he'd just poured into the child-sized plastic tub that sat in the middle of a mat on his bathroom floor. Satisfied that the water was perfect, he set Candy in the tub. She'd been a water lover from infancy, and when Donna first enrolled her in swimming lessons, Candy could already outswim a tadpole and relished her bath times. The sound of her magical laughter and enthusiastic splashes soon filled the bathroom.

Smiling at the sight—there was nothing cuter than a naked baby to Ben's way of thinking—he stepped into his bedroom and plopped down at his desk. After turning on the table lamp, he reached automatically for his answering machine and rewound its tape so he could listen to the messages he'd received during his trip to town.

With the back of Candy's head in ready view, Ben made notes of calls he should return, most of which had to do with his thriving veterinary practice. That accomplished, he reached for the phone and dialed the first number, a fellow blacksmith with whom he rotated weekends demonstrating the art of forging iron at Rowdy River, one of Missouri's theme parks. No one answered, and as Ben hung up the phone, his gaze fell on an ornate wooden plaque, hanging on the wall above his rolltop desk.

A several-years-ago Christmas present crafted by his four sisters, it sported a burned-in-wood list of all the qualities he'd once told them he sought in a wife. A tiny hole had been drilled beside each quality, just the right size to hold the golf tee Ben was supposed to insert if his current ladylove had that particular trait.

Ben had dutifully hung the plaque, but never once used the list, which was long, specific and created for the sole purpose of discouraging his matchmaking siblings. At thirty-nine, Ben was weary of their attempts to fix him up with this or that friend. But try as he would, he could not make them understand that he was not quite ready to settle down. Thus the plaque—a visible reminder from his sisters that he should be out looking.

Smiling at his cleverness in making such an impossible list, Ben absently read the first quality on it: long brown hair. He immediately thought of Jennifer Robbin, who had the prettiest head of such he'd ever seen on a woman. He remembered how Candy had grabbed a handful of those luscious curls and how soft they'd felt when he freed them. Yes, Jenny certainly had long brown hair, all right, and would earn a colored peg in the hole by quality number one...if he were rating her—which he wasn't. Nonetheless, he did put a tee in the hole next to "Must have long brown hair."

Next on the list was "Must have big brown eyes." Hmm, he thought, inserting a tee into that hole, too. Jenny had those. Boy, did she have those. Jenny again? Ben frowned. He'd just met her, for Pete's sake, and hadn't been *that* impressed. Or had he? Deliberately, he abandoned big brown eyes and moved on down to the third quality: "Must be petite." Aha! Ben thought with a nod of satisfaction. Petite.

Jenny wasn't. Not that she was large. She wasn't that, either, but she was rather tall and well built and could, by no means, be called petite.

But was petite what he really wanted anyway? he asked himself. When Ben realized he wasn't totally sure, he had to admit that he probably hadn't given that quality enough thought. Tall would definitely be better for a man of his height—much more conducive to stimulating hugs where strategic body parts pressed together just right and . . .

With a soft groan, Ben got hold of his wayward thoughts and snatched the colorful tees from the plaque. The last thing he needed in his life right now was a woman—especially one as attractive as Jennifer Robbin. Having just paid off his farm and adjacent clinic, Ben wanted a few years of financial and emotional freedom under his belt before he did any serious dating. It did not take a vertical row of golf tees to tell him that Jenny was the kind of woman who could change his mind.

Not that Ben had anything against love and marriage. He didn't, and for that reason, nervously and randomly he scanned the rest of the list. "Must love kids," he read. "Must love animals. Must be a good cook, a good housekeeper, a good money manager, and good in bed." Ben grinned at that last quality, put on the list to irritate his sisters.

Whew, he thought, reassured. Any woman would have to be a paragon to fill that bill. He'd get to batch it for a while longer after all—quite a novelty for a man who'd grown up in a predominantly female household, lived with a maiden aunt during college and shared an apartment with a couple of crazy female cousins during veterinary school.

Smiling to himself, Ben remembered the good ol' days and all the fun he'd had. He then thought of the present, and, naturally, Candy. He realized the bathroom was suspiciously quiet and her head was no longer visible.

"Yo, Candy!" he yelled. "What are you doing in there?"

"Payin'," she called back.

"Playing what?"

"Bubbas."

Bubbas? Ben leaned way back in his chair so he could get a better view inside the bathroom next door. He spied his niece standing in her tub, pouring into the now-opaque water the last drops of a brand-new bottle of shampoo, which had been sitting on the floor by his own tub. Floating at her feet was an empty bottle of the dish-washing liquid he used to wash the dog, as well as a half-melted bar of bath soap.

"Aw, Candy," he groaned, getting to his feet to join her. "What are you up to?" She squealed when she saw him and sat with a plop. Laughing, she splashed energetically, which produced the "bubbas" she'd told him about.

Though dismayed, Ben couldn't help but laugh, too, as he reached down to rescue and rinse her. But now as slippery as one of those tadpoles she could outswim, Candy was hard to catch hold of and impossible to lift. Only when he'd wrapped her in a towel did Ben feel secure enough to move her to his own tub so he could utilize the faucet there. Candy loved the subsequent rinsing she received.

Ben did not. Nervous sweat beaded his brow by the time he finally got all the soap cleared away and deposited Candy safely on the foot of his massive four-poster bed. Attempting to hold her still with one hand, Ben dug into her bag for a disposable diaper with the other.

Candy, who preferred au naturel, promptly flipped over on her stomach and scrambled to the headboard. With a yelp of surprise, Ben caught her by the ankle and dragged her back, giggling all the way.

"You be still," he scolded, or tried to. Candy wasn't fooled for a minute and reached up for him, clenching and unclenching her fists in her eagerness to be lifted. Grinning, Ben gave in. "All right. You win. You can streak for a while, but you have to promise not to tell your mom or have any accidents on my floor."

With that, he stood her on the plush carpet, only to scoop her up again when his gaze fell on what looked suspiciously like a rash on her bare skin.

Ben turned on the overhead light and examined Candy more closely, catching his breath when he confirmed the existence of angry red splotches on her lower back and dimpled bottom.

"Holy moly!" he exclaimed, eyeing the rash. Was it something she'd eaten? Worn? Bathed in? He couldn't be sure. Even more distressing, he didn't know what to put on it.

Rapidly, Ben searched through his brain for the name of someone to call for help. He immediately eliminated his mother, who lived in St. Louis, and his sisters, scattered here and yon across the United States. They would only tell Donna, thereby confirming her low opinion of his baby-sitting abilities.

For the same reason, he didn't dare call any of Donna's friends, either. Ben's own friends would be no help. Most of them were single, and the ones who weren't would never let him forget it. That left only Jennifer Robbin, a virtual stranger, who would certainly know what to do and had already volunteered to help...several times.

That decided, Ben dug out her card and reached for the phone.

"Help."

Though Jenny's caller did not identify himself, she recognized his resonant voice the moment she heard it.

"What's wrong?" she demanded with a quick glance at the wall clock hanging in her kitchen, where she now worked. It was eight-thirty. Ben had been alone with Candy for over two hours. Anything could have happened, and knowing the mischievous toddler, undoubtedly had.

"Candy's got some kind of rash," Ben said. "Any idea what I should put on it?"

"You're asking *me?*" Jenny responded. Using her shoulder to hold the receiver against her ear, she unplugged the popcorn popper with one hand and reached for a mixing bowl with the other. "You're the doctor, for crying out loud."

"Actually, not that many of my patients get diaper rash."

Jenny bit back a laugh. "Diaper rash? Is that what you think it is?"

"Not really. Her bottom was clear when I changed her earlier. My best bet is that it's a contact rash of some kind."

"Contact with what?"

"The shampoo, I guess."

"Shampoo?" Jenny frowned.

"Or maybe the dishwashing liquid. Lord knows she was slick with it."

"Excuse me?"

At her prompt, Ben relayed an astounding tale of baths and "bubbas," ending with his theory that Candy must be allergic to something she'd bathed in.

"You're very lucky she didn't drink that shampoo instead of pouring it out," Jenny scolded, popcorn momentarily forgotten. "I thought you said your house was child-proofed."

"It never occurred to me that Candy would touch the stuff sitting beside the tub."

"The exact reason someone with a little more experience should be watching her," Jenny said, resuming her Friday-night ritual. Quickly, she filled the bowl to overflowing with the fluffy white kernels she'd just popped. "Look, Ben, I know you love your niece and want to spend time with her, but I really think it might be best if you let me take over. I'll call my landlady now. Since I was going to stay up to watch a couple of movies anyway, it won't inconvenience me if it's late when you get here."

"No way," he interjected. "Just tell me what to put on this rash and I'll leave you to your movies."

Jenny started to argue, but reached for the salt shaker instead. "I'm pretty sure I remember seeing a tube of ointment in her bag. See if you can find it."

There was a moment's quiet on the other end of the line and then, "Here it is."

"Good. Spread a light amount on the affected area," Jenny said, sprinkling a not-so-light amount of salt on the popcorn.

"Will do," he said, adding, "Thanks, Jenny Wren. I promise not to call you again."

"My last name is Robbin," she told him. "And I want you to call me again."

"Oh?"

"If you get in a jam," she hastily explained.

"Oh." He sounded almost disappointed. "Well, good night."

"Good night."

Deeply involved in the second movie of the two she had rented, Jenny fumbled for the phone when it rang several hours later. "Hullo."

"Help."

Jenny glanced at her wristwatch. Midnight. Surely he'd put Candy to bed hours ago. "What's happened now?"

"Candy just ate some dog biscuits," Ben said. "I know they're not poisonous, but, as you pointed out this afternoon, her stomach is delicate, and I—"

"You fed that child dog biscuits?"

"Of course not!" he snapped, obviously irritated. "She climbed out of bed, sneaked off to the kitchen and—"

"She climbed out of her baby bed?" That was quite a feat—even for Candy Monkeyshines Oakes.

"No, she climbed out of *my* bed. Her bed is still at the other sitter's."

Jennifer groaned. "You actually put that child in a regular bed and thought she'd stay there?"

"I sincerely hoped she would since I'm dead on my feet. Obviously I was wrong. Now if I promise to buy a proper baby bed tomorrow, would you dispense with the lecture and tell me what to do about the damned dog biscuits?"

"Hide them," Jenny said.

"You know that's not when I meant."

Jenny sighed. "Sorry. How many did she eat?"

"I can't be sure, but I think a couple."

She sighed again. "If she complains about her stomach, give her some of the antacid drops in her bag. Otherwise don't do a thing." Jenny shook her head, still bemused by Candy's latest escapade. "I can't believe that child ate dog biscuits. They must taste terrible."

"They're really not that bad," Ben told her.

"You ate one, too?"

"She seemed to be enjoying them so much that I..." His voice trailed to silence.

"That does it. I'm going to call my landlady right now. Them I'm going to run over to Kidstuff and get one of the portable beds. Get Candy's things together. I'll be back here in an hour."

"No. She'll be fine with me. Just fine."

"Fine? In the charge of a man who eats dog biscuits?"

"I just tasted the damn thing, okay?"

"No, it's not okay. I've got a really bad feeling about this."

"Maybe *you* need the antacid drops."

"And maybe you need help with your niece."

"What I need is a good night's sleep, which I'm probably not going to get. Luckily, tomorrow's Saturday. Thanks for your help, Jenny. You won't hear from me again."

"Hello?"

"I lied."

Jenny looked at the clock beside her bed. Six a.m. So he'd survived the night with his niece...a major miracle. "What has Candy done now?"

"Nothing. Well, nothing worth telling, anyway." There was a moment's silence and then, "Can you hold on a minute? Candy's raised the lid on the toilet and Flicka's getting himself a drink."

"Flicka?"

"The cat."

He had a cat named Flicka? Jenny shook her head in disbelief and waited.

"Still there?" Ben asked seconds later.

"Still here."

"Good. What I called about is—No, honey. Don't pull Flicka's tail. You'll hurt him." Ben sighed heavily. "Still there?"

"Still here."

"Good." He hesitated. "Where was I?"

"I'm not sure," Jenny replied. "But I think you were just about to tell me why you called."

"Oh yeah. Mike Stone, the blacksmith who switches weekends with me at Rowdy River, just phoned, and he's— What are you doing?"

"Excuse me?"

"Not you. Put the kitty down, honey." Jenny heard a yowl in the background. "Candy, no! You're supposed to *love* the kitty."

Jenny grinned.

"Still there?"

"Why did you call, Ben?" she asked.

"Because you told me to if I got in a jam and I'm in one, or Mike is. He sprained his wrist playing tennis yesterday—needs me to fill in for him today."

"And you want me to keep Candy, is that it?"

"Yes. I'll pay you double whatever you usually get."

"I don't 'usually get'," Jenny told him, oddly miffed. "And haven't, since I was a teenager trying to earn pocket money. As manager to all three Kidstuff day-cares in Springfield, I do very little actual baby-sitting. When I volunteered to keep Candy last night it was strictly as a favor to her mother."

"And her mother will thank you...if she ever finds out," Ben assured her. "Now about today, my road is a mess, so I'd better come get you."

"Hold on a minute," Jenny said, irritated by his assumption that she would drop everything and come to his aid. It was one thing to help out because he needed her, quite another to help out because he had something else he'd rather do. "This is awfully short notice—"

"But you said you didn't have any big plans for the weekend."

"And I don't, but I still have some things I—"

"Holy moly! *Candy, no!*"

"What's wrong now?" Jenny asked, tensing.

"She's kissing Flicka."

Flicka? Who'd just sipped from the toilet? Jenny's stomach lurched.

"You win. I'll keep her," she said with a sigh of resignation. "But at my place instead of yours. Surely I can get by with it for a day."

Chapter Three

"Why risk getting in hot water with your landlady when I have a better idea?" Ben replied. "You and Candy go with me to Rowdy River today. While I do my demonstrations, you two can enjoy the rides, check out the crafts and snack on funnel cakes. You *have* tasted funnel cakes, haven't you?"

Jenny certainly had, and her mouth watered at the very thought of sampling another of the sugar-sprinkled confections Rowdy River boasted.

Suddenly, visiting the park didn't sound like such a bad idea, and not just because of the delectable sweets. Krissie hadn't exaggerated last night when she commented that Jenny's administrative job limited her time with the tykes she loved. Jenny couldn't remember when she last looked after a toddler one-on-one for more than a few minutes, which meant her baby-sitting skills were probably a little rusty and no match for the likes of Candy Oakes. Rowdy River, full of plenty to keep a child entertained, might prove a godsend until she got her confidence back.

Besides, Jenny always enjoyed the park and hadn't visited there in over a year. "I love funnel cakes, actually."

"Good. Come with me today and I'll buy you a dozen," Ben responded.

She had to laugh. "A dozen would make me fat, not to mention sick."

"So I'll buy you one funnel cake and one frozen lemonade and one bag of curly fries and . . ."

Jenny groaned. "Hush. My stomach is reminding me that I haven't had breakfast yet."

"Then I'll buy that for you, instead. They've got freshly ground sausage, country biscuits and gravy, eggs—whatever your heart desires—at the Blue Plate Café. Come on, Jenny Wren. Spend the day with me."

"With Candy, you mean?" she asked, suddenly breathless at the thought of spending a day with the handsome persuader on the other end of the line.

"Right. With Candy."

Jenny hesitated, then deliberately shrugged away her lingering doubts. A day at Rowdy River sounded wonderful and could only be fun, especially with a child along. "Well, okay. Why not?"

"Thanks," Ben said, a note of triumph and maybe just a little relief in his voice. "I'll make it worth your while, I swear. Now, I need to be at the park by eight-thirty and it's a good twenty-minute drive. Can you be ready by, say, eight?"

"I can be ready," Jenny told him, already tossing back the pastel blue sheet that covered her, and swinging her feet to the throw rug on the hardwood floor next to her bed. "My address is on the card I gave you yesterday. Do you need directions?"

"I'll find it," Ben assured her.

"All right then. I'll see you at eight."

But she didn't see him at eight . . . or at eight-thirty, either. In fact, the clock said 8:42 before Ben wheeled his truck in front of her apartment and screeched to a halt. Jenny didn't wait for him to get out but stepped outside and locked her door. Motioning for him to stay put behind the steering wheel, she hurried to the truck and squeezed in beside the car seat, mounted near Ben's right elbow and filled to overflowing with a beaming, bouncing Candy.

"Sorry," he growled, as he reversed the truck and then sped down her street.

"You couldn't find my house?" Jenny asked.

"I couldn't find Candy's toy, and she wouldn't leave without it."

Jenny glanced down at the toddler, who clutched a well-worn teddy bear. "What have you got?" Jenny asked her.

"Beah," Candy replied, quite solemnly.

"And what is your bear's name?" Jenny asked. "Yogi?"

Candy shook her head so hard her curls bounced.

"Pooh?"

Another enthusiastic denial.

"Hmm." Jenny made a great show of thinking, her eyes on the faded brown bear with its black button eyes and sagging pot belly. She'd never seen it before. Odd, she thought, since Candy clearly loved it. "It must be named Smokey."

Candy huffed her exasperation with the two thick-headed adults. "No, no, no."

She's certainly got that word down, Jenny thought, trying not to smile. "Then I give up. What in the world is your bear's name?"

"Tigga," the child promptly replied.

"You named your bear Tigger?" Jenny asked, her thoughts naturally turning to the Christopher Robin stories and his mischievous stuffed tiger of the same name.

Candy giggled and shook her head again, but did not enlighten her questioner. Baffled, Jenny looked over the child's mop of curls to Ben, catching his attention and then arching an eyebrow in silent questioning.

"The bear's name is *Trigger,*" he said, immediately shifting his gaze back to the road.

"Trigger?" Jenny questioned in amazement. "As in Roy Rogers and . . . ?"

"That's right."

"And I thought *Tigger* was an unusual choice for a bear." She shook her head, baffled. "Why do you suppose she named him that?"

"*She* didn't, actually," Ben said. "*I* did . . . when I got him for my fourth birthday, thirty-five years ago."

"The bear belongs to you?" For the life of her, Jenny could not picture Ben as a child, dragging the animal along behind, even though its tattered paws and threadbare ears were solid proof he must have.

Ben flushed. "I only keep him around for Candy."

I'll bet. "Well then, why did *you* name that poor bear Trigger?"

"Because I really wanted a horse for my birthday."

Jenny laughed. "Your parents wouldn't buy you one?"

"No, and they wouldn't let my grandpa, either."

"Uh-oh," Jenny teased. "Do I detect a note of bitterness . . . and after thirty-five years?"

Ben shot her a glance, then shrugged rather sheepishly. "I really wanted a horse."

"You don't think four is a little young for that kind of responsibility?"

"Nope," Ben replied. "I was born in the saddle—" he glanced at a dubious Jenny "—well, maybe not *born* there, but I took my first ride when I was fifteen months old, and—"

"You're kidding!"

"I swear," Ben told her with a cocky grin. "'Course I was sitting on Grandpa's lap at the time. . . ." His voice trailed into thoughtful silence. He looked down at his niece and playfully tugged a lock of her hair. "Candy, here, loves horses as much as I do. Don't you, honey?"

Momentarily enthralled by Ben's wristwatch, Candy did not reply.

Grinning, Ben let her pull the timepiece over his hand and place it on Trigger's arm. After kissing the top of her head, he huskily added, "And if she wants a horse when she's four, I'm going to get it for her. Sooner, in fact, if a deal I'm working on right now comes through."

Jenny never doubted that for a minute, and touched by the depth of Ben's devotion to his niece, barely heard his next words.

"What about you, Jenny Wren? Do you ride?"

"Hmm? Oh, uh, no. I'm a city girl." She deliberately ignored the nickname, his second use of it in the past few minutes. Something told her if she made a fuss it would most likely follow her to the grave.

"Tough luck," Ben said as he rescued his watch and slipped it back on. "Maybe I'll just enlighten you to the joys of country living while I've got you—I mean got *her*—this week."

Disgustingly thrilled by the hint of promise in those carelessly uttered words, Jenny shifted her gaze away from Ben and out the window. She gave herself a mental scolding for her utterly female reaction to a male who could probably lay claim to each of the undesirable characteristics on her list and maybe even a few not on it.

What was it about Ben that reduced her from a mature, man-proofed woman to a sweaty-palmed bimbo? His twinkling eyes? His killer smile?

No, not those, Jenny decided, though both might be lethal to any other woman.

No, it was something else altogether: Ben Ryder's attachment to his teddy bear. That startling sentimentality, so unexpected, so atypical of the men Jenny knew, attacked each and every prejudice she harbored, thereby threatening the philosophy of a lifetime.

Clearly, she would have to watch her step with this one. He could mean big trouble to her precious independence.

That acknowledged, Jenny took a deep, calming breath and a good look at the passing scenery, which was not exactly what she'd expected.

"Where are we going?" she immediately demanded, realizing they were several blocks past the turn to the highway and, eventually, Rowdy River.

"Springfield Rental. They close at noon, and late to work or not, I've got to stop and pick up a portable baby bed and a high chair."

"Wise move," Jenny murmured.

"I thought so," he agreed with a grimace, turning the truck into the parking lot of a vast shopping center. He hopped from the vehicle without another word and disappeared through a glass door, only to step back out in a matter of minutes, a high chair tucked under one arm and a fold-up baby bed under the other.

In record time, the items were loaded into the back of his truck, protected by a camper shell. And exactly twelve minutes after their arrival at the rental store, Ben headed his truck out onto the street once more.

"Will you get in trouble for being late to work?" Jenny asked, when they'd backtracked to the highway that would take them to the theme park, and they'd made the critical turn.

"Work?" Ben laughed. "Smithing is more play than work, at least for me. As for getting in trouble... since I'm the only blacksmith around today, I don't think anyone's going to be in a rush to fire me. Besides, I'm not really late—at least not for my first demonstration. That doesn't start until ten-thirty. The head honchos just like for us to be in place as soon as the park opens so we can visit with our guests. And speaking of guests... what's this guest's favorite attraction at Rowdy River?"

Jenny thought for a moment. "The Glass Gallery, I think. I find the glass blower particularly fascinating."

"I could introduce you to him," Ben teased. "He's a friend of mine."

"Actually I was referring to the craft, not the man," Jenny retorted.

Intrigued by her dry response to his joking offer, Ben made the most of this opportunity to find out more about her. "What's the matter? Already have a man in your life?"

"No."

"Oh?"

"And I like it that way."

"Oh." Ben noted his keen disappointment, a startling reaction considering his determination to avoid serious involvement with the fairer sex for a few more years.

Serious involvement? Ben frowned. Now why on earth would a term such as "serious involvement" pop into his bachelor brain—and in relation to Jennifer Robbin? For the same reason he'd compared Jenny's attributes to those on that damn list back at home the night before?

It looked that way. And that meant he'd better watch his step today and every day until Donna got back and his life returned to normal. Something told him Jenny might not be as easy to relinquish as his niece.

On that ominous thought, Ben spotted the employee entrance to the park. He glanced at the clock on the dash, noting it was now nine-thirty. He was an hour late, a fact he hated in spite of what he'd told Jenny, and there was still much to do to ready his smithy for the day.

The second that Ben parked the truck and killed the engine, he bounded out of it and ducked back inside for Candy. "We can go in this gate, here, which will take us by the office," he told Jenny. "I've already obtained permission for you to roam at will, but we need to check in...."

"Ben—"

"Then we'd better go to the public entrance so we can rent a stroller...."

"Ben—"

"*Then* I'll take you two to the Blue Plate—"

"Ben!"

"What?" he asked, startled by Jenny's near yell, inches from his ear.

"I'm perfectly capable of doing all those things alone. Don't you think you should clock in—or whatever it is you do—before those 'head honchos' you mentioned come looking for you?"

Ben hesitated, then gave her a grateful grin. "Yeah, I guess I'd better." He kissed Candy on the tip of her up-turned nose. "Bye, kiddo. Be good for Uncle Ben." His eyes met and held Jenny's. Impulsively leaning in just a little farther—and nearly squashing his niece—he managed to place a kiss on Jenny's nose, too. He saw a flicker of surprise in her wide eyes, but she said nothing. Encouraged by that, Ben naturally wondered how she'd react to a kiss on those pretty red lips.

He never found out.

Candy chose that moment to protest his proximity, a muffled wail that reminded him she might need to breathe.

"Sorry, sweetie," he murmured, dipping his head as he hurriedly backed his body out of the truck. He dug into his pocket for the two twenty-dollar bills he'd stashed there earlier and handed them to Jenny. "If you need me, I'll be at the blacksmith shop between the gristmill and the ice-cream parlor."

"I won't need you."

Jenny's no-nonsense reply told Ben she wasn't near ready for mouth-to-mouth experimentation. So with a sigh of regret and a promise to be finished by four o'clock, he retrieved his cowboy hat from the truck, shut his door and left them.

Jenny watched Ben stride toward the gate. Her gaze traveled the length of him, head to toe and back up again, lingering on his long legs and nicely rounded tush.

Not bad, she thought, immediately scolding herself for the errant thought. As a rule, Jenny didn't stare at men's behinds or at any other part of their anatomy. She left that revolting practice to women such as her mother and Krissie.

Jenny opened her door and got out of the truck. After freeing Candy, she took the child, the bear and the diaper bag in her arms and headed to the gate and what she hoped would be a fun day. She found the office easily, and after informing a secretary of her arrival, Jenny made her way to the public entrance and the rental strollers Ben had mentioned.

She spotted them right away. So did Candy, who took one look and screeched her protest. "No, no, no."

"I take it you don't want to ride in the stroller," Jenny commented, more to herself than to the tearful child. She shifted Candy from one arm to the other, mentally measuring the toddler's weight and that of the diaper bag, hanging from her shoulder by its strap, against her own strength. Jenny acknowledged that while she could carry them both for a while longer without too much trouble, a whole day of it was out of the question. "I'm going to wait an hour or two before I get the stroller," she told Candy. "Then you're going to have to ride. Understand?"

Candy nodded as though she did.

Not fooled for a moment, Jenny got her bearings and directed her steps to the music gazebo, where a man played the hammered dulcimer for a captive audience. She stole a second to relish the haunting melody, then moved on, soaking in the lazy atmosphere of the park, a scaled-down replica of an 1880s town, complete with costumed "residents."

As usual, Jenny felt as though she'd truly stepped back in time. She scanned her immediate surroundings, taking note of the cleanliness and order of the area. Though only one of thousands visiting the park at that moment,

Jenny felt neither rushed nor crowded, a fact she attributed to the rambling layout and the tall trees, which gave her a sense of solitude, while providing cool shade from the sun and unseasonably high humidity.

The smooth asphalt walk underfoot and frequently posted maps only enhanced her wanderings and, encouraged, Jenny moved on to the Blue Plate Café and the breakfast Ben had promised.

Jenny found the simple country fare delicious, and so did Candy, who ate her pancakes with gusto. After washing the toddler free of maple syrup, Jenny changed Candy's diaper at the "baby station" in a nearby rest room. Then the two of them began some serious exploring.

They visited the candy factory first. Jenny, too full to sample the taffy, nonetheless loved to watch it being made. So did Candy, at least for a split second. Then she was ready to move on.

Jenny wisely didn't argue. Shifting her squirming bundle to the other arm, she backed out the door the way she'd come in and walked to the next attraction, the glass gallery she adored. But one step into the shop, filled to capacity with every shape and price of dainty glass trinkets, Jenny had serious second thoughts.

What woman in her right mind would take an octopus such as Candy Oakes into a place like that? she asked herself, leaving again with a regretful sigh and a promise to come back some other time... alone.

By now, both her arms ached, and no amount of switching off could alleviate the agony. Jenny pivoted and, with quick steps, made her way back to the front gate. Whether she wanted to or not, Candy had to ride in a stroller. Jenny couldn't carry her one step farther, and according to the clock in the town square, it was only 10:40. They had hours to go before closing time.

As expected, Candy protested—loudly—when she realized their destination. Embarrassed, but determined, Jenny utilized some of her fast-returning baby-sitting skills and cajoled the child with a hastily created explanation that the petting zoo was too far away to walk. Surprisingly, her tactic worked, and momentarily encouraged by Candy's cooperation, Jenny dug into her pants pocket for the rental fee.

She paid and picked out a sturdy metal stroller with four wheels and a large compartment for the bag and any purchases. There was a seat belt, too. Certain she was going to need that, Jenny set Candy on her feet by the stroller and turned her attention to figuring out the seat belt, which someone had left badly tangled. Then Jenny reached for Candy.

But the child wasn't there.

With a gasp of fright, Jenny stood and whirled, her anxious eyes searching the immediate area. She glimpsed her energetic charge, highly visible in a bright red romper, just disappearing into Kiddieland . . . at a dead run.

Jenny ran, too, pushing the cumbersome stroller ahead of her. By the time she entered the play area, fenced by split railing, her blouse clung to her back and sweat trickled between her breasts. Not pausing to catch her breath, Jenny abandoned the stroller and forged ahead, scanning each and every child-sized ride and attraction for Candy.

Seconds that seemed an eternity later, Jenny spotted the curly-headed toddler, elbows propped on the knees of an elderly lady, who sat on a bench. Obviously delighted by her companion, the gray-haired woman listened intently to Candy's nonsensical chatter.

Relief washed over Jenny, relief so intense her knees threatened to buckle. Now sucking in that much-needed breath, she slowed her steps and closed the remaining distance between them. Candy saw her and waved, her big, dark eyes asking *What took you so long?*

With a wry smile, Jenny reached for her. "Don't ever do that again," she said, giving her a hard hug that belied the scolding.

The child returned the embrace, adding a kiss—or the eighteen-month-old equivalent of same. She didn't pucker up, exactly, but Jenny had relished enough pint-sized kisses to recognize one when lucky enough to receive it.

Her heart melted—but not completely.

"Ready to ride?" she asked.

Candy shook her head.

"Too bad," Jenny murmured under her breath. She gave the obviously amused woman a quick smile, then headed back to the stroller, luckily still parked where she'd left it minutes before.

Though Candy stiffened in initial resistance when Jenny lowered her into the stroller, she quickly accepted that this time there would be no escape. With a surprisingly grown-up sigh, the toddler settled into the seat and pointed to the petting zoo, several yards ahead.

Smiling in spite of herself, Jenny pushed the stroller in that direction, and for the next half hour they petted and fed woolly lambs, cuddly rabbits and waddling, quacking ducks.

They also rode the carousel, or Candy did. Jenny stood beside her, secretly clutching the back of the tyke's romper so she wouldn't fall off. As Ben had said, Candy clearly loved to ride and urged the ornate wooden horse to go faster.

At the thought of Ben, Jenny glanced at her watch, noting it was almost noon. Did he stop to eat? she wondered, on that thought pushing the stroller to the nearest map. A quick perusal revealed that the blacksmith's area wasn't so very far away, and not really sure why, Jenny headed in that direction.

She slowed her steps the moment she spied the rustic lean-to and halted at the edge of the crowd so Candy would not see her uncle and call out to him. Jenny noted that he'd donned a bibbed leather apron and now stood before an open fire. The dancing blaze shed a golden glow over his flushed face when he moved to shift a rectangle of red-hot metal from the flames to a nearby anvil, via a pair of long-handled tongs.

Magnificent muscles rippled against the thin cotton shirt with every fluid motion as he next raised his hammer. Metal clanged against metal; sparks flew. Without taking his eyes from his work, Ben explained the process of forging a hunting knife, his current project.

Hit hard by the sheer sexuality of the man, so handsome, so strong, yet so boyishly caught up in his work, Jenny suddenly rued the curiosity that had brought her to his corner of the park. But entranced, she made no move to leave. Instead, she handed Candy a graham cracker from her bag to keep her occupied, then turned her attention back to Ben and his steady monologue.

"My grandpa...was a...blacksmith," he told his enraptured audience between hammer blows. "I spent every summer on his farm from the time I was two until he died, when I was nineteen. I learned the craft from him."

"Is this what you do for a living?" a tall redheaded youth in jeans and cowboy boots asked.

"No. I'm a veterinarian, actually," Ben replied with a grin. "And I have to credit my grandpa with that, too. He loved all animals, especially the horses brought to him for shoeing. He passed that love on to me."

"Got any of those knives you're making, for sale?" asked a curvaceous female, who looked to be mid-twenties. "I know someone who'd love to have one."

"Your husband?" Ben asked, winking broadly to the others in the group.

"My boyfriend, actually."

"And how big is this boyfriend of yours?"

"Six foot five, two-twelve."

Ben winced. "In that case you'll find several of my knives in the general store, about a hundred yards south of here."

"What would you have answered if I'd told you that my boyfriend were five foot two?" the woman quizzed, obviously basking in Ben's attention.

"Why, then I'd suggest we meet over dinner and discuss arrangements for a special order."

She laughed good-naturedly at that, as did all the onlookers.

Jenny didn't find Ben's antics nearly so amusing, and she glared at him. As though feeling the heat of her censure, Ben suddenly raised his gaze over the heads of his companions to lock with hers.

His face immediately split into a grin of delight. He waved and, to her dismay, directed the attention of everyone to her and Candy. Face flaming, Jenny was forced to make small talk with each and every one of Ben's newfound friends as they dispersed and wandered away.

"What a precious little girl," the last one, a petite woman, said, kneeling to inspect Candy eye-to-eye. "She looks like her daddy."

"I think she looks like her mother," a man, most likely her husband, commented. Jenny's face flamed when she realized he'd focused his appreciative gaze on her.

"Oh, I'm not—"

"Hi ya, honey," Ben said from behind her.

Jenny abandoned her intended denial and turned, expecting to see Ben's eyes on his niece. But they weren't. "Uh, hi," she replied rather coolly.

"She's probably mad at you," the woman teased, rising to shake a finger at Ben. "You're a shameless flirt."

"Isn't he, though?" Jenny murmured.

"Oh, I wouldn't worry," the woman hastily added, as though she feared Jenny might. "He's obviously crazy about you." At that, she flashed a warm smile, which included them both, and took her husband's hand. "Your demonstration was so interesting," she told Ben as she moved away. "I'm going right now to get one of those knives for my dad's birthday."

"Thanks," he murmured to her retreating back.

"'Hi ya, *honey?*'" Jenny said, the moment she and Ben were alone with Candy.

He laughed away her irritation. "I could tell she thought she had us figured out, and I didn't want to embarrass her."

And what about embarrassing me? Jenny wanted to ask. But she didn't.

Ben unknotted the red bandanna looped around his neck and knelt to wipe Candy's face. "I see you've just eaten a cracker. Was that dessert or a little tide-me-over until lunch?"

"We haven't had lunch," Jenny told him.

"Then why don't I take a break and join you two ladies?" he suggested, scooping Candy up out of the stroller before Jenny could reply.

"Where's your hat?" Jenny asked, noting how his hair gleamed blue-black in the sun.

"In the shed. I thought that it might be best to take it off." He glanced down at his Western-style clothes, then grinned. "It might be a bit much with the rest of this getup. Women can't resist cowboys, you know. I wouldn't want to cause a riot."

"In your dreams," Jenny muttered, a comment that produced a laugh from Ben.

Clearly unperturbed by her insult, Ben shook the crumbs from his bandanna and put it on. That accomplished, he stashed the stroller in the lean-to and led the way to an outdoor restaurant, where they dined on barbecued chicken, roasted corn on the cob and baked potatoes, all cooked in an open pit.

A short hour later found the two females on their own again. Since the toddler looked exhausted, Jenny found a grassy knoll sheltered by trees and they sat down to rest. A quick glance skyward revealed the reason for the sultry air—storm clouds had gathered in the southwest and now covered most of the sky.

Jenny took Candy in her arms and offered her the bottle of juice reserved for naps and bedtime. The child took it, and as hoped, quickly nodded off. Jenny took advantage of the quiet to lean against a tree and do some dreaming of her own—daydreams about a baffling blacksmith with a ready smile and a soft heart.

There was no doubt about it. He seemed to be the man of her secret, never-verbalized fantasies. He seemed to be a man she could love. He wasn't of course, but for the first time in a long time, Jenny actually questioned her decision to live her life alone.

Had that decision been made too hastily, based on the rejection and pain of another woman—her mother?

But of course not, she ruthlessly reminded herself. That decision had been made based on a list of male traits, painstakingly compiled through the years from first-hand experience. And though Ben seemed to be different from any man she'd ever met, she knew better than to believe it.

Still...

Jenny huffed her impatience with herself. Why the sudden doubts? she wondered. Why this unexpected willingness to let Ben prove he wasn't like all the others?

And what made her think he'd even want to? A total stranger's observation that he was "crazy" about her?

"Tigga?"

Jenny started and looked down at Candy, now wide-eyed and wide-awake.

"Tigga," Candy demanded, sitting up.

Jenny scanned the ground around them, then glanced at the stroller. No bear. Thinking back to lunch, Ben's demonstration and even the petting zoo, Jenny could not remember the last time she'd seen it.

Her stomach knotted. She leapt to her feet and stashed the empty bottle in the diaper bag.

"Where is Trigger?" she asked, just as a drop of rain splashed onto the asphalt a few feet away.

"Gone, gone," Candy told her solemnly and without hesitation.

"Gone where?" Jenny persisted.

Candy thought for a moment. "Hebben."

"Heaven?" Jenny echoed in horror. "Did you say 'heaven'?"

Candy nodded confirmation, then added, "Poor Tigga."

Chapter Four

Jenny spent the rest of her afternoon pushing the stroller, dodging scattered rain showers and retracing steps in a frantic attempt to find Ben's bear, but to no avail. The bear was lost—well and truly lost.

Sick at heart, she finally gave up the search and sat down on a bench situated within smelling distance of a funnel-cake booth. Candy, entertained by the breakneck speed at which they whizzed through the park in the past few hours, quickly grew restless. She stood as though to climb out of the stroller.

"Sit down," Jenny said, her patience with everything worn quite thin.

"No, no, no," the child retorted, looking for all the world as though she might burst into tears.

Jenny, close to doing the same, skillfully utilized a time-tested tear-allaying tactic—diversion. "Want to watch how they make funnel cake?" she asked hopefully, just as someone walked by holding a paper plate heaped with the goody.

Candy, who probably didn't even know what one was, nonetheless nodded eagerly.

"All right," Jenny murmured. With a definite lack of enthusiasm, she stood and pushed the stroller the few steps to the booth. She lifted Candy and let her watch as the woman inside, dressed in a long calico dress, poured batter from a container resembling a funnel into a huge cast-iron pot filled with hot oil.

She swirled the batter as it poured, creating loops of crisp, golden-brown cake. At just the right moment, she scooped the cake out of the vat and let it drain before placing it on a paper plate. She then sprinkled powdered sugar all over.

"Mmmmm," Candy said, sniffing the air like a puppy.

Jenny had to smile. "Want to share one?" she asked even though she knew she couldn't choke down a bite. All she could think about was Trigger, Ben's cherished bear, gone for good.

Jenny paid for the sweet. Dragging the stroller behind, she and Candy returned to their bench, where the toddler consumed a healthy portion.

"So here you two are. I should have known you'd be close to the funnel cakes."

Jenny looked up at the sound of that familiar voice. "Yeah."

"Is something wrong with it?" Ben asked, joining them on the bench to eye what remained on the plate.

"No," she said. "I'm just not hungry. Want my share?" She offered it to him.

He took it and made short work of eating all but one bite, which he tried to give to Candy, now sitting in his lap. She wrinkled her nose and pushed it away with a firm shake of her head and a "Yuck."

Ben hooted with laughter. Jenny didn't crack a smile.

Frowning, he swallowed the last morsel and licked the sugar from his fingers. "Tired?"

"Very."

"Well, I came to tell you that we can leave anytime. I don't work in the rain and the crowd has thinned, anyway."

He got to his feet. Jenny reached out and caught his sleeve, halting him. "Ben, something's happened. Something awful."

He tensed. "What are you talking about?"

She stood, tipping her head back slightly so she could look him dead in the eye. "It's Trigger. We lost him."

Ben opened his mouth to blurt, "So what?" but caught himself just in time. Jenny's worried frown told him she sincerely believed he cared for that silly old bear. Her use of "we" said she intended to take full blame for its loss. Having spent a solid hour that very morning looking for that very bear, Ben knew who the culprit really was, and Jenny's loyalty and concern touched him.

"I've looked for him all afternoon," she continued, actually wringing her hands in agitation. "I've retraced every step we've made today. He's gone, Ben. I'm so sorry."

"I take it Candy couldn't tell you where she left him," he murmured to let her know he didn't blame her for what had happened.

Jenny shook her head. "Candy tells me he's in heaven."

Ben choked back a laugh. Heaven? Trigger Bear, who'd been a willing accomplice to untold mischief through the years? Fat chance. Unbidden, unexpected, childhood memories suddenly washed over Ben. At once, he wished he'd said goodbye to that ol' bear, a regret that surprised and embarrassed him.

"Well, there's no use crying over spilled milk," he gruffly proclaimed to hide his emotion. "All I know to do is check the Lost and Found when we leave. Maybe he's been turned in. It's a cinch nobody would want to keep him."

"There's a Lost and Found?" He heard the hope in Jenny's voice.

"At the front gate by the stroller rental desk."

Grasping the handle of Candy's empty stroller, she set off at a near trot in that direction. Ben, Candy in his arms, caught up with her in two long strides and they quickly covered the remaining yards to the desk, where he turned in the stroller.

The three of them then approached the Lost and Found booth. Ben's stomach twisted with what could only be anxiety. Shaking his head in disbelief at his sappy sentimentality, Ben described the bear to the attendant. She told them to wait, left the desk, and returned seconds later . . . holding Trigger.

Candy squealed her joy, a sound Ben could easily have echoed . . . if he weren't a grown man of nearly forty. He allowed himself nothing more than a smile, hoping Jenny would assume it stemmed from pleasure at his niece's happiness. Jenny laughed her own relief, and to Ben's surprise gave him—Candy, Trigger and all—a hug he felt clear to the bone—and a few other critical places.

He hugged her back with his free arm, boldly adding a kiss right on those pretty red lips that had haunted him all day. Jenny pulled away almost instantly and ducked out of the embrace, but not before his pulse rate tripled.

"I'm so glad we found your bear, Ben," she said in a perfectly normal tone of voice, as though nothing had transpired between them.

Ben knew better. So did his thudding heart.

And so did Candy, who laughed with delight. "Nuh-Ben sugar!"

Sweet, sweet sugar, he silently added, waiting for Jenny's response, which he hoped would tell him the kiss had hit her even half as hard.

She merely held out her arms to the toddler. "Ready to go? I know Uncle Ben's just dying to give you another bath, and I've got a few things to do today, myself."

Put in his place, Ben heaved a mental sigh and led the way to the employee's entrance, where he checked out. They were almost to his truck when someone called his name.

He stopped and turned to see one of the secretaries, running after them. It seemed he had a message to call Ralph Edison, the vet with whom he swapped weekend calls.

Ben groaned, knowing Ralph would never phone unless it was important. After a quick explanation, he handed Jenny the truck key and made his way back to the office.

Jenny had Candy secured in the car seat by the time Ben joined them again. His dragging step and sagging shoulders told her something was wrong.

"What is it?" she asked, the minute he climbed behind the wheel.

He gave her a long look, then shook his head. "Ralph's wife, Heather, has gone into premature labor. I'm going to have to assume on-call duties for the rest of the weekend, and I've already had an urgent summons from Clark Kennels. I've got to get over there right away."

He leaned forward to rest his forehead on his hands, clenched around the top of the steering wheel. After drawing in a couple of deep breaths, he sat back and looked her square in the eye. "I know you've got things to do, but do you think you could keep Candy just a little longer?" His pleading eyes and hopeful half smile set her whole body atingle.

Freshly reminded of his shocker of a kiss moments ago—she'd tingled then, too—Jenny knew she'd be wise to refuse his request. But how could she? The man had big problems, and she, of all people, fully understood his reluctance to leave such a mischievous toddler with someone who didn't know or love her.

"I'll call my landlady right now and get permission for Candy to spend the night," she told Ben as she reached for the door handle. "We can stop by your place now and get her things."

"But I don't have that kind of time. Please stay at my house until I return. I swear I won't be long."

"I suppose I could. . . ."

"Thanks, Jenny Wren."

"But there is a condition."

Ben eyed her warily. "Which is?"

"Stop calling me Jenny Wren."

"You've got it," he promised with a laugh of relief.

Jenny said little during the ride to Ben's place, and since he and Candy were as silent, she had plenty of time to wonder why she'd given in to his pleas so easily. Sure, she felt sorry for him, but there *were* limits to human kindness. . . .

Was his crazy, unexpected kiss the reason? she wondered, immediately banishing that theory to parts unknown. Ben's kiss had nothing to do with anything, least of all her decision to help him out.

Was it, then, because he intrigued her so?

Possibly, she thought, for there was no denying he did that. Why, she couldn't say. He was just another man... or was he?

Jenny's thoughts naturally jumped back to Candy's nap time, earlier that afternoon, when similar speculations about Ben filled her head. She'd wondered then if he were different from other men. She still wondered.

Why? she asked herself. Why assume for one second that Ben couldn't claim each and every manly characteristic on her list? Was it because he'd demonstrated that he wasn't selfish, item number two on that list?

Maybe, she decided. For all his faults, Ben Ryder could never be called selfish. Hadn't he given up a whole week so Candy wouldn't have to stay with strangers? Hadn't he worked at Rowdy River for his friend, Mike, and wasn't he now taking weekend calls for another friend, Ralph?

And since he didn't deserve that label, could it be he didn't deserve to be called spoiled rotten, manipulative, arrogant or preoccupied with sex, either?

Yes, she realized, her heart sinking. And that's why he intrigued her, and *that's* why she'd agreed to help him out tonight. She wanted to get to know him better.

How she wished she'd just told him no instead, and retreated to the safety of her apartment. If she never found out that he was a man she could love, she wouldn't risk losing her heart. Above all, Jenny didn't want to lose her heart, for experience had shown her that losing one's heart ultimately meant losing one's identity.

Be careful, she warned herself. *Keep your distance.*

Rain had begun to fall in earnest by the time Ben deposited Jenny, Candy, the baby bed and the high chair at his house. After promising to cook them all a steak on his return, he drove down his private road into the night. Jenny headed straight to the bathroom he'd pointed out. There, she expertly bathed and dried the droopy-eyed toddler.

When Jenny finished dressing Candy in a T-shirt and diaper from the bag, she fed her a bowl of cereal and milk. That accomplished, Jenny located the den, the television and the children's channel.

Candy managed to stay awake a whole ten minutes before she gave in to fatigue and fell asleep on the couch. Smiling at the toddler, so deceptively angelic in peaceful slumber, Jenny scooped her up and deftly deposited her and her precious bear in the baby bed Ben had set up in a bedroom down the hall.

Resisting the urge to further explore his house, Jenny walked back to the den. She did let herself check out every nook and cranny of that room, decorated in a contemporary style, and lined with richly paneled walls, built-in bookcases and a huge stone fireplace. At one end of the room she saw a sliding glass door. Closer inspection revealed a wooden deck outside, complete with hot tub and cedar patio furniture. Beyond the deck lay rolling lawn, towering trees and, several yards from the house, another building she assumed must be Ben's animal clinic.

Behind the clinic, just visible through the trees in the waning light, Jenny spied long animal runs, enclosed by a tall chain-link fence. Everything looked spotless to her critical eye—from the den to the runs outside—a fact that impressed her. Most men weren't so neat.

Another difference? she wondered, even though "sloppy" wasn't checked off on her standard list of miserable male mannerisms.

Jenny next perused Ben's bookshelves and smiled with pleasure when she found a whole set of Sherlock Holmes mysteries. She selected one of her favorites and retreated to the couch, where she whiled away a couple of hours, one ear tuned to Candy, one ear tuned to the thunder that rumbled with increasing frequency. She still sat there when Ben finally returned home shortly after seven o'clock.

At the slam of the kitchen door, Jenny rose and headed that way. There she found Ben, standing in a growing puddle of water. His pale blue shirt, soaked and clinging, accentuated the planes and angles of his chest, the strength in his arms. Duly impressed by his physique, she let her gaze drop to his jeans, plastered to powerful thighs and calves, and then to his sock feet.

"Lose your shoes?"

Ben gave her a weary grin and shook his head. "Left them on the porch. Ellen would kill me if I tracked up the kitchen."

"Ellen?"

"My housekeeper."

So much for differences.

"Where's Candy?" he asked, stepping to open a door at one end of the kitchen. Jenny saw that it led to a laundry room. Ben walked in and pulled off his socks, which he tossed in the open washing machine. He began to unbutton his shirt.

"Um . . . asleep," she blurted, naturally wondering if he intended to shed *all* his wet clothes right there.

"Good," he murmured, untucking and slipping out of the shirt to reveal his broad, muscled chest, lightly sprinkled with curly dark hair. Ben then gave the shirt a toss and reached for the buckle of his tooled leather belt.

Jenny gulped and turned her back on him, scurrying to the door under the pretense of looking out into the dark.

"Still raining?" she asked in a voice too loud. The next moment she gave herself a mental kick. Unless he'd spent the last few hours playing in the sprinkler, it was definitely still raining.

"Pouring, actually," Ben replied from right behind her.

Jenny caught her breath and turned to find him scant inches away, holding the belt, still wearing his jeans, and grinning as though he knew the topsy-turvy state of her hormones.

She cleared her throat self-consciously and took a giant step back. "I've, um, always loved stormy weather."

"You and my ducks. Frankly, I wish it would stop—at least long enough for me to get this damn road paved." He draped the water-spotted belt over the back of one of the four chairs surrounding the kitchen table, then ran his fingers through his drenched hair, a move that sent silvery droplets sailing everywhere. "I know you're probably starved, but I've got to get out of these wet jeans. I'd really like to take a shower before I start dinner, too."

"You don't have to cook for me," Jenny quickly interjected. "All I've done today is eat, and at your expense." She dug the remainder of Ben's forty dollars from her pocket and laid it on the table.

He barely glanced at the wad of bills and change. "Since Candy's asleep and I can't take you home just yet, you might as well let me feed you one more time. Unless you want me to wake her. . . ?"

Jenny definitely didn't. "Oh no. Don't do that." She deliberately kept her gaze above Ben's chin, and for that reason noted little lines of fatigue around his eyes. Obviously last night with Candy and today at the park had caught up with him. "I'll stay and eat."

He smiled that sexy smile of his. "Good. Just give me five—make that ten—minutes under the shower, and I'll be a new man."

Jenny, dazzled by the flash of those even white teeth, couldn't find anything wrong with the old one—until he left her. Then she came abruptly to her senses.

With a groan of disgust, she slapped her flattened palm to her forehead. She paced the room with agitated steps, silently bemoaning her present confusion. Was it the result of some latent gene she'd inherited from her mother—a gene that *would* show up now when she'd resigned herself to the role of bachelorette?

"Jenny?"

She whirled to find Ben standing in the doorway, watching her. "Hmm?"

"Want something to drink while you wait? There's a bottle of wine somewhere around here."

Wine? Now wasn't *that* just what her befuddled brain needed? "No thanks."

He turned to go.

"Wait, Ben. Do you need any help?"

He pivoted to face her and leaned against the doorjamb, eyes twinkling. "Well, I don't know. The shower's kind of small for two. . ."

Jenny blushed clear to her toes and looked quickly away, as stunned by his response as her vivid mental picture of them standing close under pulsing water. "I meant preparing dinner."

Ben sighed. "Just my luck." His hot gaze swept her from head to toe and back again, where it locked with hers. As though sensing her increasing disquiet, he asked, "Did I shock you?"

"You embarrassed me," Jenny told him. "I'm not used to being teased."

"Who's teasing?"

"You'd better be," she replied.

His expression never changed. "And if I'm not?"

"The baby-sitter is out of here now—rainstorm, sleeping child or no."

Ben stood in silence for a moment, as though taking measure of her desperate bluff. Jenny held her breath while she waited for his response, knowing that if he made one move to test her resistance, it would all be over and tomorrow would find her just another fool-hearted woman lost in a man's world.

So much for being careful. So much for keeping her distance. Jennifer Robbin wanted Ben Ryder and that's all there was to it. God help her if he figured it out.

"In that case," he finally murmured. "I guess I am teasing... this time, anyway. And if you really want to help, you'll find salad makings and steaks in the refrigerator and a loaf of French bread in the pantry."

Weak-kneed with relief, Jenny nodded and shooed him out of the kitchen. Though a lousy cook, she knew she could throw together a salad and slice the bread. That would keep her hands occupied until she came to her senses or he got dressed, whichever came first.

She took a second to familiarize herself with Ben's ultramodern kitchen before exploring the refrigerator and digging out the lettuce, cucumbers, carrots and tomatoes she found there. Jenny deposited these on the counter, then searched for a mixing bowl, which she promptly dropped when an earsplitting clap of thunder rattled the walls. At once, intense darkness enveloped the house.

Jenny stifled a scream. Hand to her pounding heart, she made her way to the door, only to stumble over the plastic bowl. After scooting it aside with her foot, she stepped out into the pitch-black hallway that led to Candy's room. She strained her ears for the child's cry, but heard nothing except the rumbling thunder and what sounded like hail, pelting against the windows.

Guided only by the occasional flash of lightning bright enough to permeate the blackness in the hall, Jenny groped her way along. Her fingers met the door facing Candy's room. She turned and stepped through the opening just as a blinding flash silhouetted a fast-exiting Ben, who must have already checked on his niece.

He cried out as he crashed into her, then stumbled, and fell, taking Jenny right down to the plush carpet with him. She landed on her back, half in the room and half out of it, Ben sprawled on top of her.

"Are you okay?" he immediately demanded.

Okay? Lying under the long-legged likes of Ben Ryder? He had to be kidding. Her heart pounded. Her head spun. Her lungs labored. And the tempest outside had nothing to do with any of it.

"I—I think so," she nonetheless murmured.

He shifted position, then pulled away from her as though about to stand. Feeling oddly anonymous there in the dark, Jenny gave in to forbidden desire and boldly wrapped her arms around his waist to halt him.

Ben froze. Sporadic bursts of light illuminated the guest room, throwing a shadow over his face, but his ragged breaths told her all she needed to know. Eagerly, she welcomed him when he lowered his body to hers again, his weight on his forearms.

Jenny moved her hands lightly over his still-bare back. He shivered violently.

Amazed at that reaction—his flesh actually felt *hot* to the touch—she boldly explored the ridges of his spine with her fingertips. Her left hand traced a path upward to his hairline, her right dipped downward to his waist.

Ben groaned huskily in response and pressed his lips to hers in a hungry kiss the likes of which Jenny had never known or ever imagined.

So this is what it's all about, she thought, an amazingly rational observation since Ben had trailed his lips over her cheek to plant a kiss at the outer edge of her eye. Rational thought ceased a heartbeat later when he nibbled her earlobe and buried his face in the curve of her neck.

Amazingly, goose bumps danced down Jenny's arms. And though burning inside, she shivered, much as Ben had done moments before. He touched his lips to hers again...and again. She responded with abandon, matching him kiss for explosive kiss.

The rain, the lightning, the thunder—Jenny forgot them all as she melted into a puddle of submission beneath him. Her head spun, her senses reeled. Her body begged for more...until a pint-sized wail of fear suddenly pierced her haze of passion, yanking her back to the here and now.

Ben jackknifed to his feet and leapt to Candy's bed, a few feet away. While he soothed the frightened child, Jenny got to her feet on legs downright shaky. Still slightly dazed, she couldn't quite assimilate what had happened, much less rationalize it. Grateful for the dark, she left the room and made her way to the kitchen, where she stood alone for several moments, sucking air into her lungs.

Jenny then put trembling hands to her flaming cheeks, moaning her humiliation and disgust. Clearly she'd deluded herself all this time and was no different from her mother or Krissie. Faced with that truth, Jenny wanted to run away and hide where no man could find her. At the least, she wanted to lock herself in her apartment so she could think.

"Jenny? Where are you?" Ben's voice came loud and clear over the waning storm.

Wishing she could vanish, Jenny called back to him. In a heartbeat he joined her in the kitchen, a sniffling Candy and a flashlight in hand. "Everything okay in here?"

Every*thing*, maybe, she silently responded. Aloud she just said, "Yes."

"Good. Would you take Candy while I see if I can flip the breaker switch and get us some power?"

Jenny nodded and reached for the toddler, who came to her willingly and clung. Soothing Candy with soft words and hugs, Jenny watched Ben disappear into the utility room. Moments later he was back.

"It's not the breaker. I guess I'd better take a look outside." He stepped through the door onto the porch, then ducked into the pouring rain. Jenny, who could hear only an occasional rumble of thunder, realized that the storm had decreased in fury.

In seconds, Ben stuck his soaked head back through the door. He gave her a distracted smile, mumbling, "Maybe I won't need that shower tonight after all."

"I'll get a towel," Jenny said, turning.

"Check the utility room. There might be some on the dryer."

There were. Ben, now standing just inside the door, mopped his face and torso, then he reached for the phone book. Aided by the flashlight, he found the number he wanted and dialed it. A moment later, Jenny heard him report that a transformer on the power pole outside had been struck by lightning.

"Got any candles?" she asked him the moment he hung up again.

He stared at her blankly for a moment, then came to life. "Oh, uh, in the drawer, I think." Obviously disturbed about something and deep in thought, he didn't point out which drawer.

And Jenny didn't ask. "Something wrong?"

"Hmm?" He looked at Jenny without seeing her.

"Is something wrong?"

"Wrong? No, but I'd better check on my animals." He started toward the hall door, then stopped abruptly. "Do you mind . . . ?" He nodded toward Candy.

Jenny shook her head.

"You keep this," he said, handing her the flashlight. That said, Ben vanished into the hallway. A few seconds later, she heard the patio door open and then slide shut again.

With a sigh, Jenny aimed the beam of light to the kitchen table and the high chair sitting next to it. She scooted the chair over by the counter and put Candy in it before retrieving the plastic bowl from where she'd dropped it a few minutes—or was it an eternity?—ago.

She located the candles and, after setting a couple in a juice-sized glass, lit them and set to work preparing the salad. While Candy played drums on her high-chair tray, Jenny sliced the bread, and since Ben still hadn't returned, marinated the steaks in a mix she found.

She next set the table, a task just completed when the back door slid open again.

"Is there another towel?" Ben called out.

She found and tossed him one.

Jenny knew better than to watch him dry off, and looked up coolly when he finally walked to the kitchen a few minutes later and glanced at her handiwork. "Looks like you've got everything under control. Why don't I fire up the broiler, put on the meat and slip down the hall for that shower I never got?"

"You want me to cook the steaks?" Jenny squeaked. Having lived alone for the past eight years, she seldom bothered with more than salads, TV dinners, or an occasional Crock-Pot concoction.

"Please." He turned on the broiler, situated under the oven of his gas range, then arranged the steaks on a flat pan he dug out of a cabinet. After sticking the pan in the broiler oven, he gave Jenny a smile of encouragement and disappeared.

Panic welled up in her, but determined to do this thing right, Jenny ignored it. She also ignored her fluttery stomach—a last, lingering result of Ben's mind-bending kisses. Determined to forget what had happened between them, she watched the steaks closely, turned them before they were ready, and heaved a sigh of relief when Ben finally walked back into the kitchen to take over chef duties.

He'd dressed in sweats and—thank goodness—a T-shirt. Still barefooted, he looked relaxed but a little worried, an emotional state Jenny credited to his concern about the storm, his niece and his patients.

"Do you have many animals in your clinic?" she asked, handing him the long-handled fork she'd used to turn the steaks. Surely if she pretended the encounter in the hall hadn't really happened, he would, too.

"Actually my Labrador retriever, Beauty, and my cat, Flicka, are the only animals out there right now besides my rabbit."

Jenny managed a smile. "And what's the rabbit's name? Silver?"

Ben shrugged. "Peter Cottontail. I didn't name *him.*" His eyes swept the length of her, lingering where they had no business, and gleaming by the time he raised them again. At once Jenny's heart began to thud erratically.

So much for pretending nothing had happened. Clearly he wasn't going to... or let her.... Darn the luck.

Past ready to escape his gaze, intimate as a caress, she did her best to hurry him up. Finally he finished the steaks and they sat down to eat. Jenny, who couldn't have eaten a bite if her life depended on it, busied herself administering to Candy—cutting up tiny bites of carrot and steak and buttering a slice of bread. Ben ate with relish, his gaze never leaving her. The glow of the candles on the table paled in comparison to the glow in his eyes, and Jenny found herself as flustered as a teenager on a first date by the time they finally finished the meal.

Antsy, uncertain, embarrassed, she longed to go home.

"That was delicious," Ben said. "I'm surprised you haven't stolen some poor bachelor's heart."

"I'm not into crime," she told him. Then she added, "Are you finished? I hate to eat and run, but it's really late and I'm awfully tired."

He said nothing, just got to his feet, helped Jenny with her chair, then took her hand and led her to the door, which he opened. With a nod, he directed her gaze outside. "Look out and tell me what you see."

Baffled by his actions, Jenny did as directed and saw . . . water. Everywhere. Ben's porch could have been a boat dock, his yard a river. His road, once muddy, had vanished completely.

"Oh my God," Jenny murmured, horrified.

"The creek's backed up," Ben said. "You're going to have to stay here with me tonight."

Chapter Five

"You've got to be kidding," Jenny said, gaping at him.

"No. I couldn't drive you home without risking all our necks—even in my truck."

"But I can't stay here," she protested.

"Why not? I've got plenty of room, and I—"

"Ben," she interjected sharply. "I have to go home . . . now."

He gave her a pitying smile and shook his head. "I'm sorry. You can't."

"But—"

"No buts. You cannot leave tonight and maybe not even tomorrow."

Jenny's heart sank and something very like panic threatened to choke her. "But I . . . you . . . we—"

Ignoring her stammering, Ben walked back to Candy and lifted her from her high chair. "I know you just woke up," he told his niece, "but it's back to bed anyway. I'm beat and I'm sure Jenny is, too."

With that he left the room.

Jenny glanced outside again—not quite able to accept what had happened. Then she shifted her gaze to the door through which Ben had just disappeared. He actually thought she'd agree to spend the night? After what had transpired between them only a short time before? Ha!

Why, he might take it into his head to tiptoe into her room in the wee hours of the morning, thinking she would be waiting. And why shouldn't he think that? She'd acted like a hussy, instigating and encouraging their disgusting little idyll.

Jenny frowned and looked outside yet again, vainly trying to come up with a way—any way—she could escape. Hip boots? she wondered frantically. A boat?

"No amount of wishing is going to make the creek go down," Ben said from behind her.

Jenny whirled to face him. "Can't blame me for trying," she snapped.

Ben just laughed. "It won't be so bad," he said. "See, here are some pajamas you can wear tonight." He stepped back into the kitchen with a flat cellophane package that looked as though it had just come from a department store.

At her raised eyebrow, he shrugged. "A gift from my mother...years ago. I don't sleep in pajamas."

Jenny gulped audibly at that tantalizing tidbit. Certain it would be best that she not know what, if anything, he did sleep in, she snatched the package.

"Hey, I'm sorry, okay? I didn't plan this." His eyes pleaded with her.

Jenny gave Ben a last, long look, glanced at the mess outside again and abruptly gave in to the inevitable with as much grace as she could muster. Resisting the urge to stick her tongue out at him, she sashayed past Ben and down the hall, heading who knows where.

"Your room's on the left," he called after her. "Mine is on the right. We'll share the bathroom connecting them."

Share the bathroom? she thought. With that notorious shower in it? Fat chance. Once she got into the bedroom, she'd lock the door and not show her face until dawn. And if he made one move—one teeny-tiny move—to come into her room, she'd...

Do what? Jenny asked herself. Scream? Kick? Bite?

Or welcome him into her bed?

With wings on her heels, Jenny burst into the bedroom and slammed the door behind her. A quick push of the doorknob locked it, protecting her from her own self-destruction as much as from her all-too-willing partner in it.

"You're okay," she told herself aloud, between pants. "One little slipup does not an affair make. If you keep your cool from now on, he will, too. He won't have any choice."

Not believing a word of it, Jenny stepped out of her shoes and crawled between the sheets... fully clothed.

Hours later—the clock nearby said 2:00 a.m.—Jenny gave up all hopes of peaceful slumber and tossed off the pillows covering her head. She heard nothing from the room on the other side of the bath, quite a novelty after hours of bumps, thuds and baby-sized squeals, all of which told her Candy was as wild as the weather and not a bit sleepy.

That meant Ben must finally have coaxed his rambunctious niece back to sleep and most likely slept now, himself. Silently Jenny put her feet to the carpeted floor. Quietly she unlocked her door. Stealthily she crept down the hall to the kitchen and the after-midnight snack she hoped would settle her stomach and help her sleep.

An eerie glow emanated from that room. Curious, Jenny eased to the door and peeked inside to find Ben and Candy sitting in the middle of the floor. By the light of a kerosene lantern they created who knows what from a colorful pile of building blocks.

Jenny smiled at the sight, taking note of Candy's bright eyes and Ben's bleary ones. He looked two knots past the end of his rope and certainly in no fit shape to seduce...or be seduced. In spite of everything, Jenny felt sorry for him again. Marching into the room, she sent him straight to bed and took over baby-sitting duties, fully prepared to utilize every trick of the trade to pass the time until morning and, with luck, blessed normalcy.

Hours of restful slumber later—six, according to his watch—Ben sat up on the side of his bed and yawned. He felt better, he decided, flexing his stiff neck muscles. Much better...ready to spend a lazy day with his niece and, if the creek hadn't receded, the baby-sitter.

Hot damn.

Ben reached for his bedside lamp to check out the status of the electricity and grinned when the bulb glowed in response. After dressing in jeans and a T-shirt with St. Louis Cardinals emblazoned across the front of it, Ben padded down the hall in search of his guests. When a quick peek in the bedrooms did not produce them, he headed to the den.

There he found both, stretched out asleep on the carpeted floor, oblivious to the glorious sunshine of dawn. Smiling, Ben made a beeline to the kitchen, where he peeked through a window to check the weather, then put on a pot of coffee. While that perked, he drew out of his pantry everything he'd need to make the pancakes his niece loved.

Before he actually prepared them, Ben peeked back into the den. He found Jenny and Candy still dreaming, and unsure of how late they stayed up the night before, he decided not to wake them just yet.

Ben sat in his recliner instead, and reached for his remote control. He turned on the television, volume as low as possible and able to still be heard, before settling back to watch his favorite Sunday-morning fishing shows.

Though usually enthralled by the outdoor scenery and how-to tips, today Ben found his attention wandering from the wonders of nature to the wonders of the females who'd shared his house the night before. He'd had a ball and loved every minute of their company in spite of all the problems—a fact that astonished him.

Never had his house seemed so cozy, so like the loving home in which he'd been raised. Bemused, Ben acknowledged how much he'd missed the fun and confusion the fairer gender of all ages naturally generated.

His gaze fell on Jenny, sleeping so peacefully. She lay on her side, one arm draped loosely over her midriff, the other bent back to pillow her head. Ben noted that she wore no rings... at least on the hand he could see. Pale pink nails tipped each finger—nails which had trailed down his back mere hours before and driven him to the edge of control.

His body responded now to the memory of her touch. He closed his eyes, reliving their frenzied kisses, and wondered what she would do if he joined her there on the floor and kissed her awake. He didn't dare, of course. Not with Candy so near. But he would—someday soon when he and Jenny found themselves alone.

Alone? Ben frowned at that thought. Unless he made a conscious decision to pursue Miss Jennifer Robbin once Donna returned from her trip, they would never find themselves alone. Candy was the reason Jenny now shared his roof. When Candy went home, so would the baby-sitter.

That was a depressing thought, and suddenly gloomy, Ben toyed with the idea of dating again. But dating sometimes led to love, he remembered, and love to marriage. Was he ready to take that kind of risk?

Ben thought of the plaque hanging above his desk in the bedroom. He realized he could place another tee—no, two—in the holes on it. Jenny was not only a good cook, a fact proved by dinner the night before, but she also loved kids. Why else would she sit up half the night with his niece?

That left only four wifely qualities unchecked—news that made bachelor Ben Ryder a little nervous. Could it be that he was supposed to spend eternity with Jenny? he wondered, looking at her with new eyes.

Would he be swapping his precious freedom for a wedding ring sooner than he'd planned? Ben's palms grew sweaty at the very thought.

At that moment, Jenny stirred and stretched lazily, making a purring sound that did amazing things to his libido. Abruptly he decided it might not be so very bad to wake beside her every morning. Would she let him do some in-depth research on her unchecked characteristics to see if she was *the one?* Specifically, would she let him research "good in bed"?

Probably not, he thought, as bemused by that errant thought as by his attraction to Jenny. Not into casual sex, Ben marveled at his eagerness to take her to his bed. He couldn't remember feeling this way about a woman in a very long time.

"How long have you been awake?"

Jenny's question, though whispered, broke into Ben's distraction. With a start he realized he'd been staring. He flushed. "Uh, not very long, actually." *But definitely long enough.*

She sniffed the air and sat up, brushing her hair back out of her face. "Tell me I smell coffee."

Ben grinned. "You smell coffee."

"Thank God." She scrambled to her feet and headed for the kitchen, as much to get a cup as to escape Ben's gaze, too intense for comfort. How long had he sat there, watching her sleep? she wondered uneasily. Had she snored? Drooled?

Moaned his name?

At that thought, Jenny fumbled through the pantry for a mug and poured herself a cup of the steaming black brew. She took several fortifying sips before she found the nerve to open the door and face the day.

Bright sunlight greeted Jenny and made her blink. Anxiously she scanned the yard, sighing in relief when she saw the water had receded. The road, though terribly muddy, was there again and most likely negotiable to a 4 × 4 . . . thank goodness. She could go home today.

Jenny took another swallow of her drink and glanced back toward the den, wishing that Candy would wake up soon. As though in answer to her wish, Ben stepped into the kitchen, the sleepy-eyed child in his arms.

Candy yawned widely, and when Jenny greeted her, hid her face in her uncle's neck.

"I don't think she's a morning person," Ben said.

"Neither am I," Jenny warned him.

He laughed. "That's okay. I am. Nothing either of you say or do will bother me. Now how about some breakfast? Since I didn't really cook last night as promised, I decided to make up for it this morning. I'm going to make pancakes...."

"I don't usually eat breakfast," Jenny told him even as Candy pointed to her high chair and struggled to be put down.

"But you didn't touch your steak last night," he argued as he accommodated his squirming niece by putting her in the chair. "You're bound to be hungry. Besides, if you don't eat, I'll still owe you a meal. That means you'll have to stay for lunch."

Without hesitation or a reply, Jenny sat at his perfectly set table and put her napkin in her lap. She waited patiently while he prepared the pancakes, which he served with hot buttered syrup.

Jenny took her first bite more from obligation than anything else, but hunger quickly kicked in. She then ate with relish...until she realized she would have to remove another item from her list of typical male flaws—namely, "spoiled rotten."

Ben's obvious pleasure in her uncharacteristically hearty appetite could only mean he'd done his best to spoil *her* rotten.

"Jenny?"

Why? she wondered before remembering another masculine trait on that list of hers: "manipulative." Was this Queen for a Day routine really a thank-you for yesterday? Or part of some master plan to get an emotional hold on her so she would be at his beck and call should he need her again that week?

"Oh, Jen-ny."

And what about the fiery kisses they'd shared? Kisses which cheated her out of a good night's rest. What was his motive for those?

Slowly Jenny chewed and swallowed her now-tasteless breakfast. Since no brilliant answers to her questions leapt into her brain, she decided to table her decision as to whether or not Ben deserved to be labeled "manipulative."

It didn't matter anyway, she told herself. Even if he didn't have that particular attribute, he probably had both of the equally unsavory ones remaining on her list.

"Earth to planet Jenny! Do you read me?"

Jenny dropped her fork with a clatter and blushed—something she seemed to do a lot since she'd met Ben Ryder. "Loud and clear."

"Well it's about time," he exclaimed with a chuckle. "I was beginning to wonder. So what do you think?"

"About what?" she asked, reaching to cut Candy's pancake into smaller portions.

Ben shook his head and grinned. "I said that we might want to wait a few hours longer before we leave...to give the road time to dry out a little."

A few hours longer? "You don't think we can make it now?" she asked.

"I just don't know. It'd definitely be a slow go."

"I don't mind," she said, adding, "I really do have to get home."

"Then we'll try it now."

He finished his last bite and took his plate to the sink, then disappeared into the hallway. He came back moments later, wearing a pair of boots, and stepped outside, not returning until Jenny had cleared the table and washed Candy's sticky face and hands. After pronouncing the road "passable," he took his niece and carried her across the sodden yard to his truck.

Jenny grabbed a couple of diapers, snatched up her purse and moved to descend the porch steps, halting abruptly when Ben yelled her name. Two long strides carried him back to her. In one smooth motion, he lifted her up in his arms, sloshed his way to the truck and deposited her—flaming cheeks, pounding heart, and all—beside his niece.

Stunned, Jenny said hardly a word on the rough ride out. But it didn't matter. Ben couldn't have heard her anyway over the growl of the truck, which lurched, slipped and splashed its way to the nearest county road, thankfully surfaced in asphalt.

From there on she couldn't have spoken if she'd wanted to because Ben never stopped talking. He touched on everything—from a horse he hoped to buy as soon as a friend named Roy located one, to his sisters, all of whom he considered as happily married as he planned to be someday.

"Good luck," Jenny muttered under her breath, a comment she really didn't intend for Ben to hear.

"Do I detect a note of sarcasm?" he asked, to her dismay.

"Probably," she admitted.

"Why?"

"Because I don't believe there's any such thing as a happy marriage, that's why."

His jaw dropped. "How can you say such a thing? I know lots of happily married couples."

"I don't," she retorted. "In fact, most of the couples I do know are divorced. I see the ex-wives Monday through Friday mornings, the ex-husbands on Friday nights."

"Ah... at the day-care," he said with a nod.

"At the day-care."

"That explains your cynicism... and the fact that you're still single, I'll bet. You've only seen one side of the coin—the wrong side."

"A matter of opinion. Now could we please talk about something less gloomy?"

Ben shrugged. "Such as?"

"The rest of your week with Candy. I'm not sure I shouldn't just take over from here. She'll stay at Kidstuff during the day as planned, then go home with me at night. I can smuggle her into my apartment if I have to."

"No way," he replied. "I fully expect for the rest of the week to be as much fun as yesterday... especially now that I've watched you handle Candy. I've learned a lot, you know. I'm an old pro."

Some old pro, Jenny thought with a mental pout, suddenly feeling rather used. Never mind that she'd as good as begged him to let her help out with his niece. If he honestly believed he could control his situation, then he deserved any grief the week might bring as well as the "arrogant" on her handy-dandy list—one of the two attributes as yet unaddressed.

As for "preoccupied with sex," the remaining attribute, Jenny couldn't be any more certain that applied to Ben than "manipulative" did. A handful of stolen kisses, no matter how potent, were hardly enough evidence to convict the man—especially since she'd provoked them. No, Jenny needed more time with him before she could pass down a verdict on either of those last two qualities... and here she sat, in a truck headed for home.

Suddenly inspired with a surefire way to verify at least one of those check marks—the one next to "manipulative"—and get this man out of her thoughts forever,

Jenny gave Ben a bright smile. "All right, Mr. Old Pro Ryder. Have it your way. Who knows...maybe you're right. Maybe by the end of the week you'll have Candy in bed by eight every night and you can sit around reading those marvelous Sherlock Holmes mysteries I saw on your bookshelf."

"Found those, did you?" he asked.

"Mmm-hmm," she murmured absently, her thoughts on her clever plan to invite Ben into her apartment. To Jenny's way of thinking, his certain refusal would prove once and for all that he only wanted her around when he needed help with his niece. Jenny could then leave "manipulative" on her list, something she desperately wanted to do. "I'm a Holmes fan, too. My favorite movie in the world is *The Hound of the Baskervilles.*"

"Would you believe I've only seen that one once?" Ben responded as he turned his truck into the drive in front of her apartment.

"Really?" Jenny smiled her satisfaction with her ploy thus far. One second more and she'd know the truth about him.... "I have the video and I'd be glad to loan it to a fellow connoisseur. You can come in and get it now."

Ben halted the truck and grinned at her. "Why, thanks. I'll do that."

"You will?" Jenny gulped her surprise. Ruing her big mouth, and the fact that her shameful attempt to manipulate *him* had backfired, she had no choice but to usher Ben and Candy into her apartment.

Ben took one look around Jenny's living quarters and mentally poked a golf tee into the "good housekeeper" hole on his plaque back home. The spotless kitchen, visible from the immaculate living room, gave him the willies, and he wished he'd left his none-too-clean boots outside.

Jenny didn't offer him a seat, but headed right to her television set. From a case sitting next to it, she withdrew a videocassette, which she handed him.

She probably keeps them in alphabetical order, he thought as he grimly took the tape and scanned the blurb on the back of it. Candy squirmed in his arms, compromising his hold on her. Involved in what he read, Ben set the child on her feet.

"Basil Rathbone, huh?" he murmured. "I'd forgotten."

"I hope you enjoy it." Ben noted an icy edge in Jenny's heretofore warm manner and frowned, wondering at it. She'd been quite friendly just moments ago. What had happened?

"Shish! Shish!"

Ben whirled at the sound of Candy's joyful outcry—just in time to see her delve into Jenny's miniature aquarium.

"Holy moly!" he exclaimed as he thrust the videotape at Jenny and leapt to rescue the fan-tailed goldfish from its certain demise. "Candy, no!"

The toddler jumped in surprise and then wailed. Huge tears rolled down her cheeks, and at once Ben's heart melted.

"Hush now," he soothed as he picked her up, sans "shish." Guessing Candy's mischief might be the reason for Jenny's sudden coolness, he gave her an apologetic smile. "I think I'd better go. You've got a pretty place here. I'd hate to see it demolished."

To his surprise, Jenny shrugged off the latest misadventure. "She didn't mean any harm."

"Tell that to the fish," Ben said with a grimace, turning toward the door. Laughing softly, Jenny followed. She handed him the tape just before he exited.

"Enjoy."

"I will." They exchanged a long look.

Abruptly, Jenny leaned forward to place a kiss on Candy's cheek. Intensely aware of her proximity, Ben made the most of it and breathed deeply of the scent that was so distinctly Jenny.

Every hormone in his body went berserk—just as they had the night before. He wanted to hold her, to kiss her, to love her.

Love her? Mumbling a hasty goodbye, Ben pivoted and strode out the door. A second later, he put Candy in her car seat and expertly secured first her seat belt, and then his own.

Without so much as a glance toward Jenny's apartment, Ben backed into the street and headed away, driving as though the devil—or Cupid—pursued.

In spite of Ben's boast and his sincere belief that he could handle Candy, he spent a rather hectic afternoon feeding, changing, chasing and "no-noing" her. If Candy wasn't dragging all his shoes out of the closet, she was emptying the cabinet of pots and pans. If she wasn't on the phone, calling who knows who, she was standing in front of the television, pushing buttons at random.

Ben did his best to corral his niece, tried to be firm. It wasn't easy. Invariably, as though sensing she'd pushed him as far as he would go, Candy hugged or kissed her way out of trouble, sometimes adding a "Wuv Nuh-Ben" that brought him right to his knees. With a groan, he'd give in . . . again . . . and let her have her way.

He enjoyed few free moments that Sunday, and he wasted those while wondering if Jenny were, indeed, the woman of his dreams. Ben's musing did nothing for his sinking spirits. Not only was the timing all wrong for serious involvement, the lady in question didn't believe in marriage anyway.

Seven o'clock that evening found him in a blue mood, ready to make a ship-to-shore call to Donna, who had no business sunning her buns in the Bahamas while he coped with her feisty offspring. Never mind that the whole thing had been his very own idea....

Jenny glanced around her depressingly quiet apartment and peered at the wall clock yet again. Seven-thirty—exactly five minutes later than the last time she checked.

At once, Jenny rued the day she ever met Candy Oakes and that too-gorgeous uncle, who'd somehow summoned her hormones out of retirement. Lonely, miserable, she almost wished she *could* credit Ben Ryder with that last male quality on her list—"preoccupied with sex"—and not so she could verify its validity. Tonight, his kisses would be welcome strictly because they set her on fire. And as for his touch... *His touch?*

"I've lost my mind," Jenny blurted, horrified at the direction her thoughts had taken. She buried her face in her hands, bemoaning this latest evidence that she was no different from a trillion other females in the world—females born holding the latest issue of *Bride's* magazine.

Clearly she'd learned nothing from her mother's miserable love life and marriages. And if she didn't watch her step, she would find herself kneeling at Ben's feet, begging for whatever crumbs of attention he thoughtlessly scattered.

"Darn it all!" she exploded just as the phone rang. Still in a temper, Jenny snatched up the receiver and snarled, "Hello!"

"Jenny? Is that you?" Krissie's hesitant question shamed Jenny, who immediately regretted her foul mood. It certainly wasn't Krissie's fault that her head spun with unanswered questions.

"It's me," she said with a sigh.

"Are you okay?"

"I'm okay."

"Good." Jenny heard her relief. "I've been worried about you. I called every hour on the hour yesterday, and before we left for the lake this morning. Where on earth have you been?"

"Out," Jenny hedged, unwilling to admit she'd long since slipped the realms of earth and now stood on the outskirts of a Shangri-la where levelheaded young women such as herself believed in happily-ever-afters.

"Out where?" Krissie predictably persisted.

Certain her nosy friend would find out the truth sooner or later—probably sooner—Jenny sighed and admitted where she'd spent most of the past twenty-four hours.

Stunned silence greeted her admission, then, *"You spent the night with him?"*

Jenny heard Krissie's horror. "I spent the night at his house, not *with* him."

A heartfelt sigh hissed in her ear. "You scared me to death," the bubbly blonde murmured.

That didn't surprise Jenny one bit. In spite of all of Krissie's lectures on finding a man, she was, at heart, as cautious as Jenny and maybe a little more traditional. As college roommates, they'd scorned their friends who slept around so casually and vowed never to do the same.

"You should have known better," Jenny scolded.

"I'm sorry. It's just that you haven't spent this much time with a man in ages, and I..." Her voice trailed to silence. "So what do you think of him?"

"He's, um, all right."

"Just all right?" Krissie asked.

"Well, maybe he's more than all right. Maybe he's... nice."

"Nice? Is that what he is?"

"Maybe *nice* isn't the right word, either." Jenny fumbled through her brain for a word to describe Ben Ryder. Sexy came to mind immediately. Knowing better than to verbalize that particular adjective, she tried another. "He's more... sweet. In fact, he's as sweet as Candy." She smiled at her clever pun.

"Sweet?" Clearly Krissie wasn't amused. In fact, she sounded downright astonished. "I don't seem to recall 'sweet' being on that awful list of yours."

"It isn't and shouldn't be. Ben is the only man—besides your Jack, of course—I'd ever call that and I do it only because he loves his niece so much and is trying so hard to take care of her."

"And that's where you come in?"

"I'm afraid so," Jenny thoughtlessly agreed, immediately wishing she could bite off her loose tongue.

"*Afraid so?* Does that mean you wish he had more than baby-sitting on his mind?"

"Don't be silly. We're just friends."

"You swear?"

"I swear," Jenny told her, crossing her fingers to neutralize the lie, much as the children at Kidstuff often did.

"But you like him."

"Yes, I do like him." *Too darn much.*

"Then maybe Saturday will be the beginning of a wonderful friendship and, if you want, more."

"I don't want," Jenny retorted. "And if I see Ben at all next week it will be a miracle."

"Won't he drop Candy off in the morning and pick her up in the afternoon?" Krissie questioned.

"Probably, but I won't be at that particular Kidstuff until midmorning and will certainly be gone before closing time."

"Too bad."

"Isn't it?" Jenny dryly agreed, adding, "Now I hate to rush, but I've got to go."

"Keep in touch," Krissie said, a request Jenny intended to ignore for a while. Since she intended to do exactly what she told Krissie—thereby avoiding Ben Ryder—she'd have no news to share with her longtime, too-curious buddy anyway.

But Monday morning found her at Candy's Kidstuff before the doors opened. She told herself and her coworkers that she needed to catch up on some book work. That didn't explain why she jumped up from her desk and ran to her door every time a car stopped outside.

Just after eight o'clock, Jenny heard Ben's deep laugh. Goose bumps danced down her arms—just as they had when she lay wrapped in Ben's. Disgusted by her reaction, she kept her seat.

Maybe he'll be in a hurry, she thought, just as he stuck his head through her door and greeted her with a big grin.

At once, Jenny's goose bumps had goose bumps. Rattled, she could barely croak a "Hello."

"I hoped you'd be here," he said, walking right into her office. "I've just survived the longest night of my life, and I need some advice."

"So Candy Insomniac Oakes kept you awake again?" Jenny asked.

Ben hooted with laughter. "Yeah. I didn't get a wink of sleep."

Jenny's hungry eyes swept his face and then the rest of him. *I should look so wonderful after a sleepless night,* she thought. He positively oozed energy and that perpetual optimism. He also oozed so much sex appeal that Jenny wished she could take him home for an hour or two and have her way with him.

Then she'd bring him back and they'd get on with their separate lives.

Simple.

"Did Candy eat or drink anything with sugar in it before she went to bed?" Jenny asked, swallowing back the nervous giggle her crazy thoughts had produced.

"Some ice cream," Ben said from where he stood, examining each and every knickknack on her bookshelf. "And a soft drink."

"Skip one or both of those tonight," Jenny advised, trying to keep her tone professional and her eyes off the back pockets of his jeans.

"Think that'll work?" he asked, looking her way, frowning.

"I'd bet on it."

"Thanks, Jenny Wre—" He caught himself just in time. "Thanks, Jenny."

"Don't mention it."

Awkward silence followed her words. Then Ben gave her a half smile and moved to the door. "I've got to go. The clinic opens at eight-thirty."

"How do your patients ever get down that road of yours?" Jenny asked.

"I don't know, but thank God they do," he said, his smile now full-fledged. He opened the door, but instead of exiting, suddenly pushed it closed again.

Without a word, Ben strode to where Jenny sat behind her desk, openmouthed. Taking advantage of her shock, he hauled her, unresisting, into his open arms, and kissed her . . . thoroughly.

When he raised his head, much, much later, Jenny's jellied knees folded under her. She sank into her chair to keep from falling and eyed him with a mixture of alarm and, yes, excitement.

"Why'd you do that?" Jenny croaked.

"Because your kisses are as sweet as candy," he said, reaching for her again. "And I've got a bad craving."

Chapter Six

But Jenny was too quick for him. Certain she couldn't handle another kiss, she jumped up and scooted around the edge of her desk, putting it squarely between them.

"Hold it right there," she told Ben, when he started to follow.

He did as she commanded.

"I think you'd better leave," Jenny next said, in her firmest, day-care manager voice.

His jaw dropped. "But we were just—"

"Go!"

For a moment, Ben looked as though he might argue. Then he shrugged and walked slowly back to the door. Clearly reluctant, he opened it and left her.

Jenny sagged with relief when the door closed behind him, knowing for certain that she couldn't have withstood temptation if he'd refused to take no for an answer. Inordinately depressed by Ben's irresistibility, Jenny sat back down at her desk and stared at the open ledger before her.

The numbers written on it danced about, refusing to be added, subtracted or analyzed. With a snort of disgust, Jenny closed the book and pushed it away.

She rested her elbows on the desk and hid her face in her hands, willing her heart back to its normal, steady rhythm. She knew she wasted her efforts. Ben's kisses had again taken their toll. It would be hours before she got her head back out of the clouds, her feet back on the ground. Why, she might not be over him by closing time.

Actually, Jenny felt her usual sensible self by noon. Lifetime goals firmly reestablished—again—she even managed to balance her books. Encouraged with that accomplishment, she packed her briefcase around one o'clock and grabbed up her purse, intending to drive to and spend the afternoon at another Kidstuff.

Jenny exited the building, only to stumble to a stop when she spied Ben, climbing out of his truck a few feet away. Renewed desire washed over her, intense and disabling as a blow to the back of the knees. Flustered by it, Jenny struggled to maintain her composure. Warily, she eyed him. Had he sensed her near surrender? Returned to finish her off?

"Wh-what are you doing back?" she demanded with bravado she didn't feel.

Ben grinned at her form of greeting and sauntered over to her. "I had to pick up some rabies vaccine downtown. I thought I'd stop by to tell Candy 'Hi.'"

Astonishment replaced Jenny's agitation. "You actually thought you could sail in, bid your niece 'hello' and sail away... *without her?*"

He frowned. "Why not?"

"Oh, Ben." Fully herself once more, Jenny shook her head at his naiveté. "She'll throw a fit the moment she lays eyes on you."

Ben pondered that observation for a second, then gave her a sheepish grin. "You know, you're probably right."

"Of course I'm right," she told him. "Now go get your rabies vaccine. Candy will be here waiting at closing time."

"Okay." But Ben made no move to leave. Instead, he dropped his gaze to her mouth.

Jenny's newfound confidence immediately evaporated. *Surely he wouldn't,* she thought with panic anew, taking a step back just in case he *would.*

Ben took a matching step forward, his intention to kiss her now evident beyond doubt. Jenny wanted to run, to hide, but her still-shaky knees wouldn't cooperate. Helplessly she stood rooted to the spot, lips atingle with anticipation by the time he bent to lightly brush his mouth over hers.

"Nice," he murmured when he stepped back again.

Nice? Her senses reeled, and he called it *nice?* Damn the man. Abruptly, Jenny wrapped her arms around Ben's waist, tugging him closer. He resisted, then rallied, pinning her against the building with his body, framing her face with his hands and deepening the kiss. Hopelessly lost again, Jenny cooperated one-hundred percent by opening her mouth to his questing tongue.

"Nice?" she asked when he raised his head again, an eternity later.

"Damned nice," Ben amended with enthusiasm, words barely audible above the blaring horns of the vehicles waiting at the red light not twenty yards away.

Face flaming, Jenny pushed Ben away and glared at him. "This has got to stop."

"What has?" he asked, most of his attention on waving good-naturedly at their noisy witnesses.

"You know very well what."

Ben turned back to her. His gaze swept her face. He leaned forward, placing his hands on the wall on either side of Jenny and gazing down on her. "Hey, lady. That wasn't all my fault, and besides... what's wrong with a few innocent kisses?"

Innocent kisses? Thank goodness he couldn't read minds. "Several things, not the least of which is the fact that we're both too old for this sort of foolishness."

Ben arched an eyebrow in obvious astonishment. "What do you mean by that?"

"We're acting like idiots," she said, ducking under his arm and putting several precious feet between them. "We have no intentions of getting seriously involved with one another, yet here we are, kissing as though we... well... had a future or something."

Ben crossed his arms over his chest and rocked back on his heels. "So it's not the kisses you object to, but the fact that they have no purpose."

"I—I guess so," she stammered, a little disconcerted by the wording of his reply.

"Then you can relax." Ben gave her his million-dollar smile. "*My* kiss had clear purpose. It was a thank-you for saving me just now. Where would Candy and I be without you?"

So that *was* it. He still needed her help, and undoubtedly aware of the potency of his kisses, cleverly used them to keep her off balance and, therefore, at his beck and call. That meant he was not only manipulative and with a capital M, as she suspected, but damned good at it, too.

"Are you busy tonight?" Ben then had guts enough to ask.

"What?"

"Are you busy? I've got to take Candy clothes shopping when I pick her up this afternoon. I'm really dreading it, and I'd like you to go with us."

"But Candy has more clothes than any *two* children I know."

"At her home, maybe," he calmly replied, reaching out to free a strand of hair that the breeze had blown to her lip gloss. She pushed his hand away.

"You don't have a key?"

"Nope," he replied, hooking his thumbs through the belt loops of his khaki trousers.

"What about the clothes Donna packed for this week? Surely that other baby-sitter is back from Texas by now and—"

"No!" Ben's sharp rejoinder told Jenny he'd already considered that option. It also told her he didn't intend to risk having his niece snatched away. "I have to get new ones and that's all there is to it. I need your help to make sensible selections."

In spite of her irritation, Jenny felt flattered. She could certainly be a help to this man, so endearingly foolish for his niece. Why, there was no telling what he might buy if she didn't go along, and no telling how much he'd pay for it. She owed it to Donna, if not Ben, to assist him.

Yeah, right.

"What time?" she asked with a heavy sigh, thankful he wasn't a salesman. Spineless wonder that she was, God only knew what she'd buy from him.

Ben beamed at her. "Five-thirty?"

"Can we make that six?"

"The stores close at seven, but if you think we can do it all in an hour—" Obviously *he* didn't.

"All right, then. Five-thirty. I'll meet you in front of Mother Goose Children's Shop."

"But Crawford's Department Store is having a sale—"

"Crawford's, then."

"I have a better idea. Why don't Candy and I just pick you up—?"

"We meet, or I don't go, dammit!"

Ben blinked in surprise at her vehemence. "There's no need to get hostile."

Oh, yes there is, Jenny silently argued, giving herself a swift mental kick for being such a wimp. Thank goodness her mother wasn't around to hear this. And as for Krissie...

Jenny winced at the thought of what that very vocal friend would have to say.

Ben drove away minutes later. Jenny got into her own vehicle, her gloomy thoughts still on her mother, who'd do anything for any man and at *his* convenience. Clearly, Jenny had no more smarts than her parent did, at least concerning the opposite sex.

How embarrassing—especially in light of all those lectures on assertiveness and independence dished out through the years. Obviously Jenny hadn't listened to her own advice, and now it was too late....

Too late? Not by a long shot, Jenny corrected herself. Ben might have snowed her this afternoon, but that was the last time. How did she know? Because she'd avoid future problems by never, ever helping him again after tonight.

At the mall much later that day, Jenny stopped her pacing and glared at the digital time, alternating with the temperature, displayed on the bank sign next door. Her own temperature shot up several degrees when she realized another ten minutes had passed and with no sign of Ben.

In a little over an hour the stores would close.

Jenny did not intend to be standing around when that happened. Uttering a very unladylike curse, she stalked to her car, impulsively pivoting at the last second when she spied a telephone booth at the corner of the parking lot.

With determined strides, Jenny walked over to it and picked up the phone. A few moments later, she hung it up again, baffled by the news that Candy still waited at the day-care. Knowing for a certainty Ben would never stand up his niece, Jenny reached for the phone book, found the number for Ben's clinic and dialed it.

"Ryder Animal Clinic," a female voice cooed.

"This is Jennifer Robbin. May I speak to Ben, please?" Jenny asked, picturing a buxom blonde with false eyelashes. Was *she* the reason the good doctor hadn't showed up? Jenny wondered, flabbergasted by a stab of what could only be jealousy.

"I'm sorry. Dr. Ryder can't come to the phone. May I take a message?"

"Yes, you may," Jenny coolly replied. "Tell him I'm waiting at the mall and Candy is waiting at the day-care. We're both getting a little impatient."

Jenny heard muffled voices, a distinct "Holy moly!" and then, "Dr. Ryder said for me to tell you he's had an emergency. He says he's really sorry he forgot the time and asks if you'd pick up his niece at the day-care for him."

At once contrite, Jenny quickly agreed, adding, "Tell him not to worry about a thing. I'll pick her up."

Another silence and then, "He says, 'thanks,' and he wants to know if you'll take her shopping, too."

Jenny sighed. "Yes, I'll take her shopping."

"That's great. He says he'll pay you back. Oh, and Ms. Robbin?"

"Yes?"

"He wants me to ask if you'll pick up a bucket of chicken on your way out to the house."

Through clenched teeth, Jenny managed a cool, "All right." *Give the man an inch,* she thought as she slammed down the receiver, her remorse scattered to the four winds.

Minutes later, Candy greeted Jenny with her usual squeal of joy. Jenny's heart melted, as it always did, and actually looking forward to their time together, she drove quickly back to the mall, where they shopped until they dropped.

Jenny, that is. Candy didn't drop. She bounced...from store to store, clothes rack to clothes rack as the two of them checked out bargains.

The task should have been easy enough—the store brimmed with marked-down summer merchandise, after all. Unfortunately, every time Jenny found what she considered a darling, reasonably priced outfit, Candy shook her head, pronouncing it, "Gwoss."

Invariably, she would then show Jenny what she preferred, usually something far less practical, far more ruffled and much too expensive. Eyeing her opinionated charge with new respect, Jenny finally let Candy do the picking out—within reason, of course and only if the price, fabric content and washing instructions passed muster.

Finally, purchase in hand, Jenny dragged her feet and her energetic companion to the cash register, where several customers waited, one of them with a little girl about Candy's age. That toddler's mother looked every bit as weary as Jenny felt, and it was with mutual, unspoken sympathy they set their two children side by side to play while they stood in line.

Jenny handed Candy her car keys to keep her occupied, then with that reassuring jingle ever in the background, turned her full attention to the harried salesclerk, hard at work figuring the various percentages to be taken off the original prices.

When the clerk finally finished ringing up the sale, Jenny charged her purchases and took the bulging shopping bag. She reached down for Candy, only to discover that the other little girl now sat alone, Jenny's car keys in hand.

With a groan, Jenny deposited her bundle on the counter, retrieved her keys and anxiously scanned the store. She remembered Rowdy River and the last time Candy had vanished. How easy it would be for someone to snatch that darling, friendly child.

Jenny's heart twisted with fear. "Candy!" she called, panicked. "Where are you?"

"He-ah," came the reply from somewhere in the vicinity of the nearby jewelry department.

Jenny hurried in that direction, exhaling her pent-up breath when she spied Ben's niece. "What are you doing?"

"I shoppin'," Candy told her, raising a chubby hand to show Jenny the heavy gold bracelet she'd selected.

"I sure hope you marry a rich man," Jenny murmured, returning the bracelet to the table from where it had come. That accomplished, she scooped up the tyke, snatched up her purchases and headed out the door before any other disaster could happen.

With every minute that passed in the next busy hour, Jenny renewed her pledge to resist Ben. She'd gone far beyond the call of duty, she told herself, and she'd done it knowing he used her. Only a fool, or a woman in love, would hang around under those circumstances.

Jenny was neither.

Dusk found a very determined Jenny maneuvering Ben's badly rutted road and drive. Soon after that, she and Candy stood at Ben's door. When he didn't answer their knocks, Jenny decided the clinic might be her best bet. Fried chicken, shopping bag and Candy in tow, she rounded the corner of the house, and approached the white frame building a few yards away.

Jenny heard chimes when she walked into the reception area of the clinic. A second later, Ben stepped into the room from a hallway to her left. He barely acknowledged Jenny's presence in his eagerness to take and hug Candy, reaffirming her theory that he only wanted Jennifer Robbin around when he needed help with his niece. She actually wondered if he'd planned this whole "emergency."

When Ben finally said hello, Jenny responded with a stony nod.

"I've got to go check on my patient one last time," he said, seemingly oblivious to her mood. "Then we'll go to the house and eat."

"Actually Candy has already eaten," Jenny told him. "She was so hungry that I fed her a drumstick and a biscuit at the restaurant. As for me . . . I really need to run. I would like to see your patient, though. Do you mind?"

"I don't mind."

With mixed feelings, Jenny set down her bundle and followed Ben into a hallway.

"You'll have to be quiet," he warned Candy, before opening a door marked Authorized Personnel Only. He motioned Jenny inside.

"What happened?" she asked when she spied the object of Ben's concern, a beautiful miniature collie. The canine, swathed in bandages, looked to be heavily sedated. Jenny's tender heart ached for the animal and for Ben, who hovered nearby, obviously concerned.

"Car hit her," he said softly, handing his niece to Jenny. He lifted the dog's eyelids, then tested the tightness of the bandages.

"How bad is it?"

"A broken leg, a concussion, some cuts and bruises," Ben replied. He rubbed his eyes, then pinched the muscles at the back of his neck.

"Who are her owners?" Jenny asked, highly conscious of the droop of his shoulders and the lines of weariness around his dark eyes, both of which told her he'd given his all the past few hours.

Ben shook his head. "Don't know. One of my neighbors found her about half a mile down the road."

Surprised to hear that, Jenny gave him a long, searching look, then moved closer and reached out, gently stroking the sleeping dog's head with her free hand. So Ben had taken in a stray and operated on it for hours, knowing he would not be compensated.

How could she be angry with this tenderhearted, generous man so unlike any she'd ever known?

And how could she possibly resist him?

Ben noted Jenny's obvious concern for his patient and sensed a deeper, warmer emotion he couldn't quite fathom, but felt to the bone. When she blinked back tears a heartbeat later, he chalked her distraction up to worry for his patient. And distracted as he was himself, nonetheless he mentally placed a tee next to "Must love animals" on his list back at the house.

That left only two items as yet unchecked, he realized with a start: "Must be a good money manager" and "Must be good in bed." Could he assess them tonight?

"Poor ting," Candy whispered.

Ben bit back a smile and took his oddly subdued niece from Jenny. He then guided both females away from his patient and out into the hall, where he lay an arm over Jenny's shoulder. "Thanks for helping me out today. Don't know what I'd have done without you."

"No problem," she replied, shaking off his embrace and heading back to the reception area with quick steps.

Ben wondered at her sudden coolness. Was she still angry about this afternoon? Probably, he decided, abandoning his just-made plans to investigate those last unchecked qualities on his list. Obviously Jenny was in no mood for questions on her fiscal talents, a development that didn't really bother Ben. Now that he thought about it, that quality rated right up there with "petite."

He sure did want to research "good in bed," though, and *that* development did bother him since it could only mean that he'd as good as let Jenny into his heart. Ben wasn't at all sure he wanted Jenny there. Hell, he wasn't even sure he wanted her under his skin.

But she was there, all right. Nothing else could explain his hot desire to bed her or the kisses he'd stolen that day.

Jenny was heaven-sent, an angel willing to share her time and talents with him at a moment's notice...*for the sake of his niece.* Ben didn't kid himself that Jenny's feelings for him motivated her help. He knew full well they didn't. He also knew that if he didn't control his devilish lust, he would lose her, Candy or no.

Ben didn't want to lose Jenny, he wanted to get to know her better, to further explore the magic they made together, to find out if she were *the one.* That meant he had to slow things down. The next move, if any, had to be hers.

"I really have to be going," Jenny said, breaking into his thoughts.

Ben winced. "Going" wasn't exactly the move he had in mind. Was it already too late to mend his ways? he suddenly wondered, heart sinking. "But I don't even know if I like what you bought. And I haven't paid you, either."

"If you don't like what I bought, you can just take it all back," Jenny told him. "As for what you owe me... I'll give you the bill when it comes."

"I'd rather pay you now," he said, taking her hand and as good as dragging her toward the door. Jenny snatched up her bag as he hurried her along. When they reached the back door of his house, she tried to pull free. Ben ignored her attempts and stepped inside, leading her right in after him. He then headed straight down the hall to his desk and the cash he kept on hand for business purposes.

Only then did he release Jenny, and that was to hand her his niece, who lay her head wearily on Jenny's shoulder.

"How much do I owe you?" Ben asked, reaching for his strongbox.

Jenny told him.

Ben counted out the bills and tucked them into her pocket. Jenny handed him Candy's new clothes and the chicken, which he sniffed appreciatively. "Sure you won't stay for dinner? You brought it, after all."

"No thanks," she said, next handing him his sleepy niece. She moved toward the door.

Desperate to stop her escape, Ben resorted to emotional blackmail, using a hostage he knew Jenny cared for. "Jenny?"

She stopped without turning.

"I think Candy is ready for bed. I don't suppose you have time to help me clean her up and tuck her in before you go? I'm not batting a thousand in that department."

"I guess I could," Jenny murmured with obvious reluctance. She turned then and stepped into the bathroom without another word. Pleased that his delaying tactic had worked, Ben followed, handing her the toddler, a washcloth and a towel, which she put to good use wiping the remains of dinner and who knew what else from Candy's face and hands.

By now, Candy's head wagged with fatigue, her eyes drooped. Jenny walked quickly to the guest room. Ben detoured to the kitchen, then joined them a moment later, a capped baby bottle in hand. Though not at all sure of the necessity of that ritual tonight, he handed Jenny the bottle, which slipped through her fingers. Soundlessly it bounced on the carpet.

Both of them bent over to retrieve it...and bumped heads in the process. Muttering an apology, Ben straightened, as did Jenny, now standing kissably close. He swayed reflexively toward her, at the last moment remembering his vow not to rush her.

The next move had to be Jenny's, he sternly reminded himself, even as she closed the distance between them and made it.

"You're...making...me...crazy," she whispered between spine-tingling kisses to his chin, cheek and neck.

Glorying in that insanity, Ben hugged her. He relished the feel of her breasts crushed against his thudding heart, and the touch of her hands, which began a lazy exploration of his back. Ben groaned softly, hit hard below the belt by that feathery touch.

On fire for much, much more, he began an exploration of his own, covering her lips with his, telling her without words exactly what he wanted.

And inexperienced as she was, Jenny understood perfectly. Impatiently shaking off the shackles of innocence, she teased and tasted her way to oblivion. All that mattered was the moment and the magic of his hands, molding first the curve of her hip, then the swell of her breast. Those hands stripped her of suspicion and pride, leaving only raw desire.

Jenny ached for more. She wanted Ben Ryder as she had no other man. She wanted him here...now...spoiled rotten, selfish, manipulative, arrogant, preoccupied with sex or no.

Preoccupied with sex?

Warning bells sounded in Jenny's independent, oh-so-sensible brain. Lost in the fire of Ben's kiss, she tuned them out.

"Ah, Jenny," he whispered, "*I'm* the crazy one." He hugged her even harder, a move which raised her up on her tiptoes. Over his shoulder, she spied the guest bed. Though pushed against the wall to make room for Candy's portable crib, it dominated the room and Jenny's thoughts. She eyed it longingly, almost wishing the two of them could just lie together on it and...

"Bobba! Bob-ba!"

With a soft curse, Ben released Jenny. He snatched Candy's bottle up from the carpet and uncapped it.

Oh-so-grateful for the timely intrusion, Jenny backed slowly toward the door. Her gaze never left Ben, now turned to his niece and passing the bottle through the rails. Candy pushed it aside and raised her arms to him, babbling sweetly. Ben groaned his impatience, but took her.

Thanking her lucky stars for his soft heart and her reprieve, Jenny stepped out into the hall...and ran like hell to her car.

Tuesday, Jenny deliberately started her day at the Kidstuff in the southern part of town, miles from where Ben dropped off his niece each day. She couldn't bear the thought of facing him again after the way she'd teased and not followed through, behavior she found humiliating and unforgivable.

Caught up in her quest to find out if Ben were different from other men, she'd foolishly ignored her attraction to him—a near-fatal mistake. And to what end? she wondered several times during that interminable day.

Though she had convinced herself he wasn't selfish or spoiled rotten, she still wasn't sure about arrogant and manipulative.

And as for "preoccupied with sex," the last item on her stupid list, how could she call Ben that when *she* herself instigated their latest encounter?

So now what? Jenny asked herself at closing time that evening. Deep in thought, she walked to her car. Disturbed, she drove straight home, where she plopped down on her couch and wasted another hour in further quandary.

Jenny decided an apology should be first and foremost on her list of options. A firm and final goodbye should be second. And third? Forgetting Ben Ryder, of course.

"Fat chance," she murmured aloud just as her phone rang. Certain it was Krissie, and almost glad for the diversion, Jenny picked up the receiver and put it to her ear. "Hello."

"Are you okay?"

Flustered to hear Ben's voice, Jenny could barely speak. "I'm fine. Why?"

"I didn't see you today. I thought maybe you were sick or something."

Or something just about summed it up, Jenny thought, marveling at his easy acceptance of her flight the night before. It seemed as though her kisses hadn't left him as hot and bothered as she thought. Maybe an apology wasn't going to be necessary after all. "I simply worked at another Kidstuff. I manage three of them, remember?"

"Oh, yeah," he said, his relief evident.

Though certain he was just glad the baby-sitter enjoyed good health, Jenny couldn't resist finding out for sure. "And that's why you called tonight... to check up on me?"

"Actually I had two more reasons. First, I wanted to tell you that Donna called today, trying to find out why she couldn't reach Mrs. Pruitt. I told her what happened."

"And?"

"And she was ready to catch the next flight home... until I told her you were helping me out."

"I see," Jenny murmured, suspicions confirmed, apology abandoned, goodbye on the tip of her tongue. "And the other reason you called?"

"Candy's got gum in her hair. It looks like I'm going to have to cut it out."

Chapter Seven

"Don't you dare touch that baby's hair!" Jenny exclaimed, leaping to her feet. She shuddered at the thought of Ben whacking at Candy's precious curls with a pair of scissors.

"But I don't know what else to do," he argued.

"Maybe if *I* tried. . . ."

"We'll be right over." No hesitation. No argument. The phone clicked dead in her ear.

So much for telling the man goodbye, she thought—at least right away. Dropping the receiver back into its cradle, Jenny made tracks to her bedroom to get into more comfortable clothes before her company arrived.

It was almost as though Ben had expected her to drop everything and help out, she decided as she stepped into faded jeans and pulled a sweatshirt on over her head. And why shouldn't he expect that? She hadn't failed him yet, had she?

"This is it," Jenny grumbled aloud. "Absolutely, positively the very last time I help that man."

Her words echoed loudly in the room, reminding her of an earlier, similar vow. She wrinkled her nose with disgust, wondering how many more times she'd say them before Donna and Andy Oakes returned from their cruise.

A quarter of an hour later, Jenny greeted Ben Ryder with a brisk nod and a new determination to bid him adieu...for good. Taking Candy into her arms, she walked straight to the kitchen and deposited the toddler on the counter so she could better assess the damage.

Jenny cringed when she saw the bright pink blob of bubble gum, securely seated on Candy's dark hair. Though the goo could be trimmed off without too much damage, Jenny couldn't bear the thought of putting scissors to curls she knew had never been cut before.

She whirled on Ben, hovering anxiously a few feet away. "Where'd she get this stuff, anyway?"

He gave her a sheepish grin. "From a machine at the gas station." As though anticipating Jenny's scolding, he held up his hand to silence her in advance. "I know. I know. Stupid move." He shrugged. "But she wanted it."

A reminder that we don't always need what we want, Jenny sternly reminded herself. Turning her attention back to the toddler, Jenny tugged gently on the sticky mess.

Candy howled in protest.

"Sorry," Jenny murmured, glaring at Ben again. "Get me a piece of ice from the freezer over there, will you? One of the women at Kidstuff swears it will take gum out of anything."

Ben did as requested, then stood close by while Jenny tried to chill the gum into a consistency more conducive to removal.

Minutes later, she swiped her numb and dripping fingers down her jeans and admitted that plan wasn't going to work.

"I knew it," Ben muttered woefully. "We're going to have to cut her hair. Donna's going to kill me."

"It's no less than you deserve," Jenny told him, propping her hands on her hips and eyeing the stubborn glob.

"Got any scissors?" Ben asked with an I-give-up sigh.

"Will you just forget the scissors? Go watch television, or something. I'll handle this."

Ben bristled visibly. "I will not. This is my fault, after all, and unlike some people in this room—" he gave her an accusing look "—I accept responsibility for my actions."

"What's that supposed to mean?" Jenny demanded, laying a calming hand on Candy, who'd begun to squirm with impatience.

"It means I don't turn tail and run when the going gets tough... or interesting."

So he *had* noticed last night's hasty exit after all. Jenny gulped and picked up Candy, a move which effectively hid her flaming face from Ben. "I suppose you're referring to me?"

"You know darned well I am." He stepped to the side so their gazes could meet.

Jenny gulped again. "All right, I admit it. I owe you an apology for running away."

"Apology, nothing. I want an explanation. One minute you were in my arms, purring like a kitten..." He closed his eyes, clearly relishing the memory. "The next,

I heard your car starting outside. What the heck happened?"

Purring like a kitten? How humiliating. "I—It was so late, I—"

"Don't give me that."

Flustered, Jenny chewed her bottom lip, searching for words that wouldn't disclose the state of her roller-coaster emotions. She dared not reveal the intensity of her attraction to Ben until she was sure he wasn't preoccupied with sex. Why, he might make the most of her vulnerability...and not for baby-sitting purposes. "If you must know, things were getting a little too heavy. I thought it best to leave."

"I take it last night's kisses had *too much* purpose."

"Way too much."

Ben stood in thoughtful silence for a moment, then shook his head, obviously baffled. "I thought that's what you wanted."

"You thought wrong."

"But you said—"

Jenny touched a finger to his lips, silencing him. "I said we were fools to stand around kissing like two people in love."

"Love?" The words came out two octaves higher than his usual rumbly bass. "You never said anything about that. What you said was 'kissing as though we... well...had a future or something.'"

So she had. A Freudian slip? "What I said isn't important. What I *meant* is—"

"And just what did you mean?" he asked.

"I meant we should stop kissing like a couple of hot-to-trot teenagers every time we get together. It might get us into trouble. Now hold your niece for a minute. I have a book I think might help us."

"Masters and Johnson?" he called after her as she dashed to the living room.

"Dr. Spock," she retorted over her shoulder a second before she escaped through the door and hurried to her bookcase. But she couldn't find that classic and so decided to look for another volume of helpful hints for child rearing.

While she searched, she pondered Ben's comments. He'd as good as admitted the kisses he'd given her had some sort of purpose. But what? she wondered. Brainwashing the baby-sitter? Or seducing her?

Not quite ready to think about *that,* Jenny threw her hands up in exasperation. Never had she met a man so enigmatic. She didn't know what he wanted from her or what she wanted from him. Heck, she didn't even know her own purpose for all those kisses.

At least she hoped she didn't. Actually, lust seemed a pretty good possibility now that she thought about it.

At that moment Jenny's gaze fell on the book she sought. She snatched it up, checked the index for *Gum, removal of,* and a second later read exactly what to do for Candy's endangered tresses.

She found Ben and his niece looking at a photograph on the wall, their backs to the door when she returned to the kitchen. Pausing just inside the room, Jenny let her gaze dwell on this male, so sexy, so sweet, so damned annoying.

What am I going to do about him? she asked herself. At once the goodbye she'd previously considered seemed much too drastic. But so did sharing his guest bed, another option that had recently crossed her mind.

Jenny abruptly realized that until she knew Ben's feelings toward her, she might not be able to bid him farewell, after all. Not only was he that intriguing, one part of her would always wonder if attraction to Jennifer Robbin, and not the need for a baby-sitter, had motivated his actions that week.

And then there was the matter of her list and the rather undesirable male traits left on it. Though Jenny didn't really intend to base her choice of mate on a list, she still wanted to know if Ben was as different from other men as she believed.

"Is this a picture of your parents?"

With a start, Jenny realized Ben now returned her stare. She walked to where he stood and glanced at the photo in question. "That's my mother and her second husband."

He winced and gave her a long, searching look. "Her *second* husband? How many has she had?"

"Three going on four," Jenny replied without emotion.

Dead silence followed her response. Then Ben cleared his throat and shifted Candy from one arm to the other. "Did you find Dr. Spock in the living room?"

"I found something equally as helpful and I now know what will do the trick for us—peanut butter."

Ben sputtered with laughter. When Jenny didn't join in, his amusement died and his smile vanished. "You're joking...right?"

"Wrong." She walked on into the room and searched her pantry, where she found a jar of peanut butter. After unscrewing the lid and retrieving a spoon from the drawer, she scooped a generous dollop onto a paper towel. "Set Candy back on the counter, please."

When Ben did as requested, Jenny handed the child the spoon, with a dab of peanut butter still on it to keep her happy. Quickly Jenny rubbed the rest of the oily brown paste into the gum, which became slick and pliable.

Painstakingly and with a grin of triumph, Jenny peeled it, bit by bit, off Candy's curls.

"Way to go!" Ben exclaimed when she finished. "You're the greatest."

"Thanks," Jenny replied, disgustingly pleased by his casual praise. That pleasure—and her pitter-pattering heart—raised again her doubts about the goodbye she'd fully intended to make when he'd darkened her door barely an hour ago.

There was no denying Ben was special and, list or no list, might even be the man she had once believed didn't exist. What harm could there be in spending a little more time with him in order to find out? Chances were that Ben most likely would exit her life as quickly as he'd entered it the moment his sister got home, anyway.

But what if he didn't? What if he called or even asked her out? Was she ready to put the fears of a lifetime behind and risk everything for love?

Love? Was *that* and not lust the reason her knees turned to putty, her brains to mush every time he kissed her?

"Dwink," Candy said then, a gentle reminder to Jenny what peanut butter could do to the roof of a toddler's—or anyone's—mouth.

"I'm so sorry, honey," Jenny said. "Would you like a drink, too, Ben?"

"Don't have time," he replied. "Just give Candy one and we'll be on our way."

So much for spending more time with him, Jenny thought with something very like regret as she washed her hands and then busied herself pouring apple juice into a plastic cup. As before, she'd served her purpose, and as before, Ben was now ready to hit the road. If she had any sense at all, she'd say that goodbye and send him on his way. . . before he broke her heart.

"Will you be at Candy's Kidstuff tomorrow?" Ben asked when Candy finished her drink.

Say goodbye. "Yes," Jenny answered.

"And we'll see you?"

Say goodbye, dammit. "Yes."

"Great. Till then, Jenny Wren."

"Till then," she promised, ready to cry with frustration. Clearly it would take a stronger woman than Jennifer "Wren" Robbin to utter those words to Ben Ryder.

That meant there was one way, and only one way to put him out of her life for good.

Just do it.

On Wednesday, Jenny did visit Candy's day-care, but not until noon, a time of day when she was least likely to see Ben. Her strategy worked, but that night she sat near the phone. . . just in case he had another emergency.

Apparently he didn't.

Jenny split Thursday between the other Kidstuffs and spent her hours in a blue funk, alternately snapping at coworkers and then apologizing. Closing time found her gloomy and depressed, partly because she missed Ben and Candy, partly because she had only herself to blame for her misery. She'd known better than to let him into her life and yet she'd done it anyway.

Shoulders slumped, eyes directed to the ground right next to her flagging spirits, Jenny headed automatically to the parking lot that evening. Upon rounding the corner of the brick building, she stopped short, those same eyes widening with shock at the sight of Ben and Candy standing between his truck and her parked car.

Jenny's gaze swept them both. Candy looked fine, she thought, as did her irresistible uncle. Could that mean that, for once, nothing was wrong?

No emergency? No crisis? No problem?

Had Ben come by to see her because he actually wanted to and not because he needed to?

Slowly, with growing excitement, Jenny approached them. Candy reached out her arms, clenching and unclenching her fists in her eagerness to be taken.

"Well, look who's here," Jenny said to the squirming toddler. She set down her briefcase and took Candy from Ben, nodding slightly to include him in her greeting. "Are you two lost?"

"No," he replied. "And that in spite of some very confusing directions." At her questioning look, he explained, "One of the workers at the day-care gave them to me when I asked where you were."

"I see. So what's the problem?"

"Problem?"

"Why did you drive all the way over here?" Jenny asked.

Ben winced. "I guess you have had to bail me out a time or two in the past few days, haven't you?"

"A time or two," Jenny murmured, hugging her precious cargo, wishing it were someone else.

Ben leaned back against his truck, crossing his arms over his broad chest. "Tonight there's no problem . . . at least not much of one. We're on our way to get an ice-cream cone. I stopped by because Candy wants 'Miss Jen' to have one, too."

"*Candy* wants me to come?" Jenny asked, looking him dead in the eye.

He returned her gaze for a millisecond, then shifted it to the golden sunset and tall trees behind her. "That's right... Candy."

"I see." Definitely hurt, but not a bit surprised by that answer, Jenny heaved a mental sigh. How much plainer could the man be? she asked herself.

"You can leave your car here," Ben said. "We'll have you back in an hour or so."

"Sounds lovely," Jenny told him. "But I'll have to pass." She handed him his niece and picked up the briefcase she'd set on the asphalt moments before. "I have some work to do tonight."

"What kind of work?" Ben asked.

"Book work. I keep the accounts for all three Kidstuffs."

"No kidding?" He sounded genuinely surprised. That rankled. Just because she was stupid enough to jump when he said "frog" was no reason to assume she didn't have brains enough to know better...or to post accounts to a ledger.

"Thanks for stopping by. Maybe some other time..." With that, Jenny dug into her pocket, extracted her keys and unlocked her car door. Intensely aware of Ben and Candy watching in silence, she slipped behind the wheel and shut the door. A second later, she started the engine, waved and backed out of the parking lot, leaving them standing there.

"Well, hell," Ben muttered, watching the taillights of her car vanish into the dusky dark.

"Hell," Candy echoed with feeling.

Ben nearly choked. "Hel*lo* to you, too, Miss Candy. And goodbye to Miss Jen, who obviously has better things to do than eat ice cream with a bee-u-tee-ful little girl and her oversexed uncle."

"Sex'd," his bright-eyed, sharp-eared companion agreed.

Ben winced, belatedly remembering Jenny's suggestion that he watch his mouth. Though tempted to warn his niece not to say that again, he decided, instead, to make light of it. "Ready for ice cream?"

She nodded eagerly and bounced in his arms, pointing to the truck.

Laughing, Ben lifted Candy high in the air, then hugged her hard. How he'd miss this bundle of joy when she went home to her mama come Sunday. His house would be too quiet, his nights too long.

And his life? Ben glanced at the empty road down which Jenny had just disappeared, knowing for a certainty his life would be too lonely and the reason more than the loss of his niece.

So much for batching it a few more years. This brief taste of fatherhood, combined with the tantalizing taste of Jenny's lips, had ruined him. Now he had forever-after on the brain and an intense longing for a house filled with laughter and love... and the sooner the better.

The clock said seven-thirty when Ben finally put Candy into her plastic tub that night and gave her a bright yellow rubber duck, a washcloth and instructions to give "Quacker" a bath.

He then stepped into his bedroom, a few feet away, where he jabbed a golf tee into the hole next to "must be a good money manager." That left only one unplugged since he'd taken care of the others the night before when trying to keep from calling Jenny.

Ben frowned at the list, his thoughts on his bungled attempt to see her that evening. *I could have sworn she was glad to see me,* he thought, plopping down in his chair and scooting it back so he could keep both eyes on his niece. Absently he doodled Jenny's name on a scratch pad laying near the phone on his desk.

So why the refusal?

Would she have joined them if he'd rephrased his invitation and admitted that *he* craved her company, and not his niece? he wondered.

Probably not, he immediately decided, spirits plummeting. Candy was most likely the sole reason Jenny had spent so many hours with him over the past few days. But if that were true, why didn't she accompany them tonight? He'd told her Candy wanted her, after all.

To Ben's way of thinking, that meant Jenny did have homework to do. And that meant she wasn't avoiding him.

Good.

Or maybe not so good, he decided a millisecond later, glancing up at his list and then absently scribbling on the scratch pad again. Except for "good in bed"—of which he might never be sure if tonight were any indication.

Not that he put that much store in sexual experience. He didn't, and actually harbored some rather old-fashioned ideas on that score. To his way of thinking, a man and a woman should gain their experience—and skill—together.

Still...he really wished he knew if Jenny possessed that final quality on his list. While that little piece of information wouldn't matter a bit if he didn't like her, it mattered a lot since he did.

"Hell," Ben muttered aloud. "I may even love her."

"Hell-o, wub," Candy mimicked from the bathroom next door.

Ben winced. *Hello, love?*

His gaze shifted to Candy, who looked just like her mother, Donna, had at that age. Suddenly Ben was a kid again, holding that precious baby sister and watching the older three jump rope. He heard their chant: "First comes love, then comes marriage, then comes Ben with a baby carriage."

His palms began to sweat.

"Uh-oh."

Ben shook himself from his stupor and noted the *oops* written all over Candy's face. "What do you mean 'uh-oh'?" he asked her, sure he'd long since child-proofed that room. "What have you done?"

"I pee-pee."

"Aw, Candy. *In the tub?*"

Only much later, when he lay on his bed in the dark, did Ben deliberately think of Jenny again. She'd hovered at the edge of consciousness all night, of course, but now he beckoned her to the spotlight, knowing he had to reach some sort of decision about her so that he could sleep.

But no easy solution presented itself.

"More time, that's what I need," Ben said, staring at his wall where the moon had cast shadows of tree limbs outside. Those limbs swayed in the same autumn breeze that drifted through Ben's open window, cooling his nearly bare body, if not his heated thoughts of a woman with dancing eyes, silky hair and legs that went on forever.

At once Ben wondered if she would ever share his moonlit bed...if he would ever gaze deeply into those dark eyes, run his fingers through that hair, feel those long legs tangled with his.

"More time," he murmured again, vowing to make the best of the two days remaining until he lost his niece to her parents, not an easy task since Jenny would only come round if Candy needed her.

"So Candy will just have to need her," Ben said. Then he plotted the whens and whys of the hours he had left.

Friday dragged by for Jenny, who opted to work at home to keep from further alienating coworkers and clients. Miserable, lonely and hating herself for feeling that way, she wished she could drag Krissie from her English class and have a long heart-to-heart with her.

Maybe that dear friend could shed some light on her dilemma and help her decide if she'd gone and fallen for Mr. Less Than Perfect. But that was out of the question, of course. Unlike Jenny, Krissie did not have the freedom to work at home, and besides, Jenny wasn't at all sure of her readiness to share her woes.

"I told you so's" were such a bore.

Eight o'clock that night Jenny found herself in front of the television, her usual bowl of Friday-night popcorn in hand. With a decided lack of enthusiasm, she searched the schedule for one of the old movies she loved to watch.

The choices were few. Impulsively, Jenny selected a Sherlock Holmes movie from her collection and inserted it into the player. Settling herself into her chair, she glued her gaze to the screen. But her attention turned elsewhere...to a marvelous man who cherished mysteries as much as she did.

At once gloomier than ever, Jenny gazed longingly at the phone. If only he would call...even to ask a child-care question.

When the telephone actually did ring seconds later, Jenny jumped so violently that popcorn flew everywhere. Setting the bowl aside, she lunged for the phone and then made herself wait another ring before answering it. "Hello."

"Hello. Is Jenny Wren there? A desperate uncle needs her."

Jenny took a moment to relish the sound of that nickname she had once hated, before responding. "Don't tell me, let me guess. Candy has hog-tied you to the recliner and is now planning your demise."

Ben's answering chuckle tap-danced down her spine. "No, but only because I hid the rope."

"Smart move. You're catching on."

"Yeah, but I don't know everything yet, which is why I called. I rented a Walt Disney movie for Candy and I'm having a heck of a time keeping her back from the television. Just how close can she sit without hurting her eyes?"

"Actually, modern research has proved that television is not harmful to the eyes."

"No kidding?"

"No kidding."

"So my mother was wrong."

"Only about that, I'm sure," Jenny said, hoping to hear his magical laugh again.

He didn't disappoint her. "Of course." Silence followed that, then, "Guess I'd better let you go. 'Bye, Jenny."

With regret, Jenny hung up the phone and turned her attention back to the movie. She didn't bother to rewind to see what she missed. She knew it by heart anyway and wasn't really in the mood for mystery.

Romance, on the other hand, might be a welcome change of pace....

The phone rang again half an hour later.

Joyfully, Jenny snatched it up. "Hello."

"Hi. Sorry to bug you again, but there's something I forgot to ask."

Hand to her hammering heart, Jenny swallowed hard to keep her voice even. "And what's that?"

"Is it okay to wash Candy's hair every night?"

"Sure."

"Even with adult shampoo? I'm out of her kind."

"You might want to dilute it first and be especially careful to keep it out of her eyes."

"Right. Thanks, Jenny. I'll try not to call again."

"Oh, I don't mind." *At all.* "Um, how is your patient?"

"Which...? You mean the collie?"

"Yes," Jenny answered, hoping her question would produce a lengthy status report...anything to delay the inevitable moment when he hung up again.

"She's fine. I don't suppose you need a good dog? She'd make someone a wonderful pet."

"Do you honestly think a landlady who won't allow children would allow pets?"

Ben chuckled. "I don't see why not. They're a lot less trouble, let me tell you."

Jenny had to laugh. "Good point, but unfortunately she doesn't see things that way."

"You know what you need, Jenny Wren?"

"What?" she asked, basking in his teasing, intimate tone.

"A new residence to start with...a big, roomy house in the country, surrounded by acres of trees and grass."

"Now how would a single girl like me manage a place as big as that?"

"She wouldn't, and that brings me to the next thing you need—a husband."

Jenny bobbled the phone at that astonishing reply. "I believe I told you how I feel about husbands."

"About marriage, anyway, and probably with good reason."

"Very good reason. And since you can't have one without the other, you must understand that a husband is out of the question."

"But think what you're missing," Ben argued. "The stimulating conversation—"

"Otherwise known as arguments."

"The challenge of running a household—"

"Otherwise known as maid service."

"The long nights of unbridled passion...."

Besieged by visions of exactly that and with Ben Ryder, Jenny found she couldn't speak.

"What's this?" he teased after a moment of weighty silence. "No 'otherwise'?"

Jenny took a deep breath, then whispered, "Otherwise known as wonderful."

Now it was Ben who couldn't speak—or that's what Jenny assumed, since he didn't for several seconds. When he did, he sounded much like a man recovering from a near-death bout of pneumonia. "Gotta go. Thanks for your help."

Jenny stared at the phone for a full minute after he hung up, wishing she hadn't been quite so honest. Clearly she'd thrown him for a loop, and if he ever called again it would be a miracle.

But the phone rang yet again not fifteen minutes afterward. With a cry of pure glee, Jenny grabbed it. "Hello?"

"One last thing, then I swear I won't call again."

"I don't mind your calling, Ben."

"That's so?" She could have sworn she heard his grin. "I just found a bottle of vitamin drops in Candy's bag. Should I have been giving them to her all week?"

"I think she'll survive a week without supplemental vitamins. And speaking of Candy, I didn't hear a peep out of her the last two times you called. Did the movie put her to sleep?"

Ben hooted with laughter. "We watched that movie for a grand total of three minutes. The reason you haven't heard Candy is not because she's asleep, no indeed. It's because she's in her high chair, finger-painting."

Finger-painting? "You bought that child finger paints?"

"It's all right. They're washable and non-toxic."

"No wonder you asked about shampoo."

Ben laughed. "Yeah. My brunette is now a redhead."

"She's painting on paper, too, I hope."

"Oh, sure. And on her tray, her shirt and the floor. I believe I see some on the refrigerator, too, and...yes, there's some on the ceiling fan."

Jenny could just picture his kitchen. "Oh, Ben. You know what you need?"

"A wife?"

"Actually I was thinking more along the lines of a keeper, but a wife might do the trick."

"Are you applying for the job?"

Jenny caught her breath. "And if I were?"

"Are you available for interview in, say, thirty minutes? I don't think I can clean Candy up and get there much sooner than that."

"Don't bother," Jenny quickly interjected, frightened by his unexpected reply. It was one thing to secretly want Ben Ryder. Quite another to find out he might want her, too. "I'm not applying."

"I'd make it worth your while," Ben told her. "Fiscally and physically. I make a good living and I've got a bod to die for."

Jenny had to laugh at that teasing, flagrant boast. "A bod to die for?"

"Mm-hmm. You hadn't noticed?"

"Frankly, no," she lied.

"That hurts. That really hurts."

"Sorry. I'll make it a point to be more observant... if I see you again."

"What's with this 'if' stuff? You'll see me again. In fact, I could be there in ten minutes."

"You told me thirty just a second ago."

"So we'll clean Candy up when I get there."

"And get paint all over my bathroom? No thanks... and that goes for all your offers."

"You're a stubborn woman, Jenny Wren."

"And proud of it," she admitted.

"Pride goeth before a fall," he reminded her.

Or after one, she thought, intensely aware of her rise in spirits, her hammering heart, her clamoring hormones. There could be only one explanation for her agitated state—love—and she wasn't ready for it. "Then I'll watch my step," she finally answered with feeling.

Ben sighed. "Well, if you change your mind, you know where to find me. 'Night, Jenny."

"'Night, Ben."

When Jenny hung up the phone this time, she flopped back on the couch and hugged a lacy pillow to her chest. She closed her eyes, analyzing their last, incredible conversation. Twice he'd offered to come over. Twice, she'd put him off.

Why? she wondered, now regretting that she'd listened to her head and not her heart. What if he never called again or made offer number three?

Suddenly the phone rang. Pleased and unwilling to push her luck further, she threw caution to the wind. "You know, Ben, maybe you *should* come on over."

"So that's who you've been talking to!" Krissie exclaimed with a laugh of triumph.

Chapter Eight

Jenny winced. "He's, um, having trouble with his niece again."

"And that's why you invited him over?"

"What other reason could a confirmed bachelorette like me possibly have for inviting a man over?"

"That's exactly what I want to know," Krissie replied.

"Why did you call?" Jenny snapped in exasperation.

"Temper, temper. There's no reason to get your undies in a twist."

"They're not, dammit!"

"Good. And speaking of which, you keep those undies on, you hear? At least until I check out this guy you've fallen for."

"Don't you dare!" Jenny exclaimed, horrified. "If there's any checking to do, I'll do it."

"On that awful list of yours?"

"Actually, you were right about that list," Jenny murmured. "It is stupid."

Heavy silence greeted that comment. "Jenny, Jenny... have you gone and fallen for this guy?"

"I wouldn't say I've 'fallen' exactly."

"What would you say?" Krissie asked.

"I'd say I've..." Jenny fumbled for an apt description of her tumultuous feelings for Ben.

"Totally flipped?"

Familiar with Krissie's skill at drawing the truth from her, Jenny gave up. "That just about describes it, yes."

"And what about Ben?" Krissie demanded. "Has he flipped, too?"

"I just don't know," Jenny admitted. "Sometimes I think maybe he has and sometimes..." Abruptly she groaned. "I sound like a ninth grader, don't I? Worrying and wondering about what he's thinking. God, I hate feeling like this."

Krissie laughed with obvious delight. "So you are human. This is great! Just great! My very best friend in the whole wide world is in love."

"I never said anything about love," Jenny interjected.

"That's because you're in denial, a perfectly natural stage in the evolution of a romance. I went through it, myself."

"Okay then, Mrs. Experience. If this is denial, what comes next?"

"Worry," Krissie informed her, adding, "That lasts until you find out if he feels the same."

"And then...?"

"Joy."

"Joy, huh?"

"Yes, and then happiness... at the wedding."

"Wedding?" Jenny sputtered. "*Wedding?* Are you insane?"

"I guess that means I can't order the bridal bouquet just yet."

"Damned right it does. Wedding...for crying out loud, Krissie. I just met the man."

"When are you seeing him again?" her bubbly friend asked, evidently not in the least perturbed by Jenny's tirade.

"I'm not. Now I have to go, all right? I'll see you...whenever."

"And if you don't, you'd better call."

"I'll call. I'll call," Jenny assured her, hanging up the phone quickly and with relief.

She stared at the nearby bowl of popcorn, all appetite for it long gone. Is Krissie right? she wondered. Have I gone and fallen in love with Ben?

Jenny cringed at the thought, but acknowledged it would explain her behavior that week. Didn't her mother always act the fool when in love?

Jenny slowly got to her feet and moved toward the hall. Two steps later, she whirled, ejected the forgotten movie from the VCR and put it away. Once again, she started to her bedroom. She managed three steps before the phone rang again.

Eyeing it with reluctance and some alarm, Jenny actually toyed with the idea of not answering. Ben or Krissie waited on the other end of the line, and she didn't really want to talk to either of them at the moment.

"Get a grip," she told herself on the fourth ring, scooping the receiver up. "Hello!"

"Were you busy?" Ben asked, obviously picking up on her irritation. "I can call back."

Jenny sighed. Just because she was angry at herself was no excuse to snap at Ben. Never mind that he was the reason for her ire. "What do you want, Ben?"

"Actually... a favor."

So what else is new? "And what favor is that?"

"Do you remember my telling you about buying a horse for Candy?"

"I seem to recall your mentioning a deal of some sort, yes."

"Well, I just received a call from Roy, the friend who's helping me locate a good one, and he wants me to take a look at a two-year-old paint tomorrow."

"You're actually going to buy a horse for that baby?"

"Yes, and this gelding may be the one. He's supposed to be very gentle and good with kids. Of course I won't let her ride alone until she's, oh, three or four years old."

"Now *that's* reassuring," Jenny murmured with sarcasm. "And where is she going to keep this horse? Don't Donna and Andy live in Overbrook Addition, which is *not* zoned for livestock?"

"I'll keep him here on my ranch. I'll feed him, train him, doctor him—"

"Ride him?" Jenny interjected.

Ben laughed rather sheepishly. "That, too."

"And what's all this got to do with me?"

"I'd really appreciate it if you'd come with Candy and me tomorrow. I'm not sure I can handle her and conduct business at the same time."

"Why don't you bring her by here on your way out? We'll stay indoors so the Wicked Witch of the West won't see her."

"Can't do it," Ben told her. "I've already promised Candy she can go see the 'horsey.' You've got to come. Or do you have other plans?"

"No other plans, but..."

"Then join us. I'll never survive the trip without you."

"That? From an *'old pro'* like you?" Jenny deliberately stressed that, to remind him of his boast not so many days ago.

"I was actually young and a rank amateur when I said that," Ben told her. "Long nights and a few gray hairs later, I realize it."

Jenny had to laugh and from habit erased "arrogant," another trait, from the "stupid" list no sensible woman would trust more than her own gut instinct—the same gut instinct that told Jenny to give Ben her tomorrow.

As for the tomorrows after that, she wasn't sure he wanted those or if she would actually give them to him if he did. Surely time spent with Ben could only make any decision easier.

"I swear this is the last time I'll bother you. Donna comes home on Sunday, you know." Ben's words told her he'd taken her long silence as "no."

They also told her he hadn't "flipped," which meant her days with him were numbered for sure, a realization which left Jenny aching and desperate. "I'll go."

"Thanks. We'll pick you up tomorrow. Is nine o'clock okay?"

"Nine is fine," Jenny told him, already dreading the final goodbye she would have to say when their little excursion ended the next day.

The second Jenny got into Ben's truck on Saturday morning, she spotted Candy's bag on the floorboard at their feet. "Before we leave...do you have everything?"

"Yep," Ben replied.

"Maybe I'd better make sure. Did you pack diapers?"

"A dozen."

"Bottle?"

"Three."

"Clean clothes?"

"Two shirts, a romper and a sundress."

"Good grief," Jenny commented. "We're only going to... Where are we going?"

"I didn't tell you last night?" He started the engine and reversed the truck into the street.

"No."

"Sorry. We're going to Poplar Bluff."

"Poplar Bluff! That's two hundred miles away."

"One hundred ninety-one, I think," he said. "I figure we'll be there by lunchtime or shortly after." He stopped the truck, shifted into drive and arched an eyebrow at her before accelerating. "Is there a problem?"

A problem? Jenny glanced from Candy, bright-eyed and smiling, to Ben, handsome as the devil, himself. How could spending the whole day with such a pair be a problem?

"None I can think of," she replied, settling back against the seat, prepared to make the most of her last day with them.

Ben grinned in response and headed the truck to Poplar Bluff.

Glancing out the window, Jenny took note of clear blue skies and a bright yellow sun, the rays of which glorified the golds, reds and oranges of autumn.

She then glanced back at Ben, now concentrating on his driving, and Candy, strapped so securely on the seat between the two of them. For just a second, Jenny imagined they were a family out on a Saturday jaunt, a surprisingly easy thing to do considering that less than a week ago she'd claimed contentment with spinsterhood.

What a change this precious pair had wrought on her uneventful life. And how could she ever tolerate that miserable existence again?

"Off."

"What...?" Jenny frowned at Candy, who kicked her heels against the truck seat.

"Off."

"I think she wants you to take off her shoes," Ben explained. "I wonder if they hurt her feet? I had a heck of a time getting them on her this morning."

Jenny pressed on the tip of Candy's white high top to find her big toe, ascertained the shoes were not too small, but slipped them and her socks off anyway. "There. Feel better?"

"Out," Candy replied, expertly unfastening her seat belt and climbing halfway out of the seat before Jenny caught her.

"You can't get out yet," Jenny told the toddler as she quickly secured her again and scooped up a familiar stuffed bear, which lay on the seat. "Here, play with Trigger."

Candy took the toy Jenny proffered, then threw it to the floor. "No, no, no."

Jenny retrieved the bear, dusted it off and tucked it safely into the already-bulging diaper bag. "I know...let's listen to the radio. What kind of music do you like, Candy?"

"Yuck."

So much for music. "Ben? What kind do you like?"

"Anything, anything," he said, eyeing his niece with some trepidation.

Jenny began with a sound she thought would soothe—classical—and worked her way to rock. Nothing pleased or distracted Candy, whose bottom lip jutted ominously by the time Jenny gave up and turned off the radio a scant ten minutes after she'd turned it on.

"Out," Candy said again, quickly tossing away her restraint.

"In," Jenny countered, securing the belt again and adding, "It's the law." She raised her gaze to meet Ben's, but he looked away, offering no help. "How about a story? You want to hear a story?"

Candy stopped squirming long enough to nod.

"Good. Uncle Ben, tell your niece a story."

"Me...?" Ben exploded even as the right front tire dipped off the pavement. He yanked the wheel hard to the left, straightened the vehicle and glared at Jenny. "I don't know any stories."

"Surely your mother told you stories when you were a kid."

"That was a long time ago," Ben argued.

"Oh come on, Gramps, give it a shot. Tell her about the three bears. Everyone's heard that one."

He sat in silence for a moment then nodded. "Okay. Here goes. Are you ready, kiddo?"

Candy said nothing, just waited, solemn as a church mouse.

Ben cleared his throat. "Once upon a time there were three bears—a papa bear, a mama bear and a baby bear."

"So far so good," Jenny teased.

Ben narrowed his eyes in warning, but said nothing to her. "The papa bear's name was Ben, the mama bear's name was Jenny and the baby bear's name was Candy."

Candy giggled at the mention of her name.

Jenny did not. "That's not the way it goes," she said, at once a little uneasy.

"Who's telling this?" Ben retorted. "You or me?"

"You," Jenny answered rather weakly.

Ben nodded his agreement. "Now Candy Bear was the cutest little critter you'd ever want to see," he continued. "Curly brown hair—" he gently tugged a lock of his niece's "—a turned-up nose—" he playfully tweaked her similar one "—and ten pink toes...."

Candy wiggled those toes in anticipation of what he might do to them and giggled again when he promptly obliged by tickling her.

"Top," she told him, kicking at his hand.

"Okay, I'll stop," Ben said. He winked at Jenny. "And I'll get on with my story. I believe I was about to describe Jenny Bear, who was one foxy mama—"

"A *foxy* bear?" Jenny interjected.

"My goodness, yes. Tall, round where mama bears should be round, with the cutest little tail in the forest."

"Ben!"

He laughed. "And then there was Ben Bear. My what a specimen—big, strong, fierce—"

"Unbelievably egotistical."

"But smart and a good provider, too."

"If he was such a good provider, why were they having porridge for supper instead of meat?"

Ben shrugged. "Every carnivore has a bad day now and then, and the reason doesn't matter anyway. What matters is that the porridge was too hot to eat. That's why they had to take the walk." He bent to kiss the top of Candy's head. "Are you with me so far?"

"How could she be?" Jenny fussed, catching his eye. "*I'm* having trouble following you."

"I don't hear her complaining," Ben pointed out.

Jenny shifted her gaze to Candy, who did seem content enough and looked from one to the other of them expectantly. Not sure which the child found more entertaining—their banter or Ben's story—Jenny gave in. "Keep talking."

Ben grinned and obliged by continuing the colorful, if less than traditional, tale. His narrative, liberally sprinkled with sound effects, kisses and tickles produced more than one giggle from his enthralled niece.

"And then," Ben said, several miles later, "Goldilocks went into the bedroom where she found a big bed and a little bed. She—"

"Hold it, hold it," Jenny interjected. "There were three beds. A big one, a middle-sized one and a little one."

"Wrong," Ben told her.

"What do you mean 'wrong'? There were *three* beds."

"Not in Ben Bear's house there weren't."

"And just why is that?" Jenny demanded without thought.

"Because Ben Bear believes in sharing."

"Oh, he does, does he?"

"Uh-huh. And he likes having Jenny Bear in his bed at night—or any other time of the day he can get her there."

"Hush!" Jenny exclaimed, face flaming. She cast a panicked look at Candy.

"Relax. This story is way over her head—literally and figuratively."

"Thank goodness. The very idea..."

"Then you liked it?"

"Liked what...?"

"The idea."

"What idea?" Jenny demanded, thoroughly baffled and not a little embarrassed by the turn of conversation.

"Sharing a bed," Ben told her with a huff of exasperation.

Jenny's jaw dropped. *Sharing a bed?* "Excuse me, but haven't we gotten offtrack here?"

Ben laughed softly. "Didn't I tell you that Ben was a smart bear?"

"'Mart bear," Candy agreed, with a nod so brisk her curls bounced.

Jenny thew her hands up in exasperation. "Just finish the story, okay?"

He did, a few miles later predicting "they all lived happily ever after" just as a rest stop came into view. "I don't know about you two, but Ben Bear needs to stretch his legs. Care to join me?"

Both females nodded.

Ben braked the truck gradually and exited scenic Highway 60. He parked under a shade tree and reached for his niece. Soon the three of them walked to a fenced overlook surrounded by rolling hills, splashed with the brilliance of autumn.

Jenny welcomed the space and the cool breeze, which fanned her still-warm cheeks. Highly aware of her jackhammering heart and Ben's speculative gaze, which she studiously avoided, Jenny suddenly wished she'd dated more as a teenager or even as an adult. A little experience with the opposite sex would have been welcome at that moment.

He looked so good today, she thought, sneaking a peek that began at his snakeskin boots and worked its way up over faded jeans to his baby blue Western shirt and then higher. His skin glowed with health, his eyes with something else, something that took her breath. She found herself replaying his unique rendition of *The Three Bears* and his allusion to shared beds. A serious invitation? she wondered and wished, the next moment telling herself it wasn't that at all, but more of the teasing at which he excelled.

"Only a hundred and fifty miles to go," Ben murmured right in her ear.

Jenny jumped at the sound of his voice, too close for comfort. "Good," she murmured, stepping away. She looked around for Candy and found her standing in the middle of a bitterweed patch a couple of yards away, busily gathering a golden bouquet.

"This hasn't been so bad," Ben told her, obviously a little put out by her answer. Belatedly he added, "Thanks to you, of course."

"Thanks to me? *You* told the story."

"You gave me the idea."

"Maybe, but I think you'd have managed fine without me today," Jenny replied, with one hand capturing her windblown hair at the nape of her neck to keep it out of her face.

"I'm still glad you're here."

How Jenny wanted to believe that answer, which seemed to say she might have misjudged his motives for inviting her along and the sincerity of his invitation to share his bed.

At that moment, she felt a tug on her pants leg and looked down to find herself the recipient of a huge bunch of flowers.

Jenny dropped to her knees immediately and took them. "Why, thank you, Candy," she said, trying not to breathe in the pollen, which invariably produced sneezes and watery eyes.

"'Mell," Candy prompted.

Jenny wrinkled her nose in protest, but did. "Nice," she lied. "Here, Ben, you smell."

With eyes twinkling, Ben took the flowers she thrust at him. "Are we *a-l-l-e-r-g-i-c?*"

"I don't know about 'we,'" Jenny told him, standing. "But I am."

"Luckily, I'm not." Enthusiastically and with great show, he sniffed the bouquet. "Mmm. Wonderful."

Candy put her hands on her hips and shook her head emphatically from right to left. "'Tink," she said, eyeing them both as though they were crazy.

Ben hooted with laughter, scooped up his niece and hugged her. "You're right. They do stink, but they sure are pretty." He turned to Jenny. "Why don't I put these in the back of the truck with the picnic basket?"

"Picnic basket?" Jenny walked over to the truck and peered through the camper window. "There *is* a picnic basket in here."

"Of course there is. Packed by Candy Oakes and her devoted uncle, Ben, as a thank-you to Miss Jenny Wren for all her help. And if we don't hit the road, we're not going to have time to eat it, look at a horse and fish."

"Fish? I thought this was a business trip," Jenny murmured just as she spied fishing poles and an ice chest, also in the bed of the truck.

"The business part of it will take a half hour, tops. The rest of the day will be devoted to an outing you deserve for being such a jewel this week."

So he hadn't asked her along just to baby-sit. He'd planned the day—down to the last detail. Jenny glowed in the aftermath of that realization and still glowed when Ben turned his truck off the highway onto a road somewhere outside of Poplar Bluff several hours later.

On either side of the narrow, graveled lane Jenny saw horses of every shape and size, from graceful quarter horses to sturdy Shetland ponies. Ahead, she saw a two-story, white frame farmhouse and several outbuildings.

In no time, Ben parked the truck and bounded out of it. Clearly impatient to greet the old man approaching them, he then reached back inside the vehicle to release his niece, who'd decided to take a snooze about five miles back.

"Let her sleep a little longer," Jenny told him, relishing the quiet and leery of waking the toddler too soon. Ben took her at her word and made tracks to their host.

Barely five minutes later, Candy stirred and opened her eyes. Obviously refreshed by her little catnap, she quickly unfastened her seat belt and crawled into Jenny's waiting arms. After a quick diaper change, Jenny joined Ben and a man he introduced as Claude Jarrett, the owner of the ranch.

While Ben and Claude talked horses, Jenny and Candy explored the immediate area and tried out a rope swing they found. After that, they admired the horses, grazing within yards of the house. Then Ben beckoned to them.

Together, they followed Claude to the barn where the paint waited. With obvious skill, Ben inspected the horse from teeth to hooves.

"Saddle her up," Claude told him.

Ben looked to Jenny, one eyebrow arched in silent questioning.

"I'm in no hurry," she told him, amused by his little-boy excitement. Stepping back, she stood in silence, watching him saddle the beautiful horse. Ben mounted in one smooth motion and, grinning, rode out of the barn and across an adjacent field.

Man and horse could have been one, Jenny thought, admiring their grace and beauty. Like countless other women through the ages, she fell captive to the charms of this "cowboy," an appeal as old and unexplainable as time itself.

Candy was not so silent. She squealed her delight and pointed to her uncle, sitting tall in the saddle and loving every minute of it. A good many minutes passed before Ben tugged the reins and guided the horse back to the barn and his waiting companions with an easy gait.

He dismounted and nodded his approval to his host, who beamed. "Fine animal," Ben commented. He turned to Candy. "Want to try him out?"

Candy nodded and reached for her uncle, who promptly set her in the saddle. Her brown eyes sparkled with excitement. Bouncing, she urged the horse, "Go."

At that prompt, Ben handed the reins to Claude, who obliged by leading the horse, appropriately named Paint, in a circle inside the massive barn. Ben, holding Candy securely in the saddle, walked along beside them, and Jenny wished for a camera to catch their excitement.

"Want to ride?" Ben asked her, when he'd halted Paint and shifted Candy from the saddle back to his arms.

"Not today," Jenny told him.

Though Ben's twinkling eyes told her he wasn't fooled by that casual answer, he didn't press the invitation. Instead, he handed his niece to Jenny and walked back outside with Claude.

Breathing deeply of the scents of the barn—leather, hay and horseflesh—Jenny followed more slowly. There were advantages to country life, she thought, a surprising sentiment from a woman who'd never lived more than a couple of blocks away from a shopping mall her whole life long.

Outside the barn, the sun shone brightly on verdant lawns and field, white-rail fencing and a rose garden.

Jenny glanced toward the stately house, taking appreciative note of the ruffled curtains visible through each window, ivy climbing up one outside wall and a porch swing swaying in the breeze.

Nice, she thought, an adjective that reminded her of a kiss she and Ben shared not so long ago. That had been nice, too, and only the beginning of what she wanted from him. Not that she was anywhere ready for the wedding bouquet Krissie wanted to order. She wasn't. She just thought kissing Ben might be an experience worth repeating.

At that moment the object of her musings walked over and took her elbow, guiding her to the truck.

"Aren't you going to buy the horse?" Jenny asked as he opened her door and took his niece.

"Probably, but not today. There are a couple more I want to check out first." He put Candy into her car seat and fastened the safety belt.

"Where are we going now?" Jenny asked when she'd seated herself next to Candy and Ben had slid behind the steering wheel.

"Actually, I'd intended to drive to Lake Wappapello, but Claude told me he had a picnic spot even prettier than that on his 'back forty' complete with catfish pond. He told us to make ourselves at home. If you don't mind, I think we should take him up on the offer."

"I don't mind," Jenny replied, relieved they weren't going to travel very far. After her taste of freedom, Candy was none too thrilled to be back in the car seat.

Ben put the truck in motion and drove past the barn and down a dirt path that led to a wooded area several yards from the house. He maneuvered the vehicle down the root-strewn way and across another huge field, halting when Jenny pointed out a picturesque pond surrounded by wildflowers and shade trees off to their right.

Minutes later, they spread a quilt. While Ben and Candy inspected the pond, Jenny unpacked the picnic basket.

With an ever-widening smile, she extracted the items her host and his niece put in that morning. She found a stuffed dog, a rubber duck, an egg beater, a plastic bowl, a can of cinnamon and an unopened can of green beans. Under all that, she found sandwiches, chips and paper plates, which she set in the middle of their "table."

"You ought to see the size of those catfish," Ben exclaimed when he and Candy walked back to Jenny. "Man, oh man."

"Big shish," Candy added, eyes wide.

"Does that mean you two want to fish first?" Jenny asked.

"Nope," Ben told her. He dropped to his knees at the edge of the quilt and set Candy down beside him. From her nearby bag, he withdrew a diaper and proceeded to change his niece.

Jenny, watching in amazement as he made short work of the task, realized he could have done it with one hand tied behind his back—a fact that pleased her.

In spite of claims to the contrary, Ben really was an "old pro" and could've survived the day without her help.

Wrapped in a warm glow of something very like love for this man who just might want her for herself and not what she could do for him, Jenny passed around the sandwiches and cold drinks.

After lunch, they walked to the pond to fish and spent a fast-paced hour catching the biggest catfish Jenny had ever seen. As did most conservation-minded sportsmen,

Ben freed all the fish they caught save the one Candy cried for. Grumbling that he had nothing to carry a fish home in, Ben put it on a stringer to keep in the pond until the moment they left. He cautioned Candy that it might get away, then glanced at Jenny, silently assuring her it would.

That done, the three of them walked back to their quilt, where Candy promptly dug her own bottle from her bag and lay down. Two swallows of juice later, she nodded off. Ben quickly jogged to the pond and freed the catfish. He then dipped his hand into the water and returned with a tiny green water turtle, not much bigger than a quarter.

"Think she'll like the trade?" he asked Jenny.

"I'd bet on it," Jenny replied with a smile. Ben made a home for the turtle in the mixing bowl before sitting beside her on the quilt. He stretched out his long legs, leaned back on his elbows, then patted the spot right next to him. Jenny scooted closer without hesitation and lay down beside him.

"Pretty here, isn't it?" he asked, slipping an arm around her. Relishing the moment, Jenny snuggled closer and rested her head on his shoulder.

"Mm-hmm."

"See what you've been missing all these years of city living?"

"Mm-hmm." She closed her eyes and sighed, relaxing and ready to take a snooze of her own.

But Ben had something other than sleep on his mind. Placing a hand under Jenny's chin, he raised her face to his and gently brushed his lips over hers.

She opened her eyes and smiled at him, then returned the kiss—an innocent gesture that set him on fire.

With a groan, Ben rolled over, giving in to his need as he pulled her closer. When a quick check confirmed that Candy slept blissfully on, he kissed an unprotesting Jenny again and again, putting his heart and soul into each one.

She pressed her body to his, urging without words, responding with abandon that set him on fire. Ben buried his face in her neck, inhaling the scent that was so distinctly Jenny. Wild with desire, he ran his fingers over her arms, then cupped her breasts. He teased the taut tips straining against her thin cotton blouse, reveling in that evidence of her arousal.

Boldly, half expecting her to stop him, Ben swiftly unbuttoned the garment and opened to reveal her bra, the color of a blush. Jenny murmured no words of protest, but did a little unbuttoning of her own before opening his shirt, untucking it and pushing it clear off his shoulders.

Jenny raised up and pressed a kiss to the pulse throbbing in his neck, then raked her fingernails down his hair-sprinkled chest. She laughed when a muscle jumped at her touch and kissed that spot, too.

Very nearly as undone as his shirt, Ben abruptly lay back to catch his breath. But Jenny didn't allow such foolishness. Instead, she followed, gave him a toe-curling kiss, then propped her elbows on his chest, which rose and fell in his struggle to breathe.

"Kiss me back," she whispered, her face once again inches from his.

Ben did . . . gladly. "Ah, honey," he murmured. "I've wanted to do this all day."

"Me, too," she told him, punctuating her confession with yet another kiss that did more than curl his toes. Ben shifted slightly, trying to ease the sudden tightness of his jeans, then gave that up, knowing it would take more than a change in position to alleviate that ache. Unless the change in position involved the sexy, willing woman now smiling down at him.

Would she? he wondered, anxiously scanning her expression. He took note of her flushed cheeks, her kiss-swollen lips, her glowing eyes. Yes, he decided. She would.

But did they dare?

He glanced over at Candy and found her not only awake, but watching with interest.

"Holy moly!" he exclaimed, sitting up and dumping Jenny in his haste. While he fumbled with his shirt buttons, Jenny did the same with hers, keeping her back to Candy.

"Now I know why my dear brother-in-law, who hates water, was so damned eager to go on that cruise with Donna," Ben muttered under his breath, painfully reminded of two other occasions when Candy had interrupted him and Jenny. He quickly tucked his shirt back into the waistband of his jeans. "He's probably been celibate since Candy was born."

Chapter Nine

Anxiously, Ben gauged Jenny's reaction. Was she angry? Embarrassed? Ready to take flight again? Anything, anything but *that,* he thought, suddenly panicked. They'd made so much progress today....

Jenny's gaze locked with his. She said nothing for a moment that lasted an eternity, then, to Ben's astonishment, burst into laughter.

"What's so funny?" he demanded. To Ben's way of thinking, amusement was almost as bad a reaction as taking flight.

"You," Jenny replied. "Me." She reached for Candy and gave her a hug and a kiss. "And this precious, precious baby." Jenny picked up the abandoned bottle and gave it to Candy, who popped it back in her mouth and settled more comfortably in Jenny's arms, looking for all the world like she might really go to sleep this time.

Though tempted to express a different opinion of their latest disaster, Ben thought better of it. Candy needed a rest, and who knows, once she nodded off, he and Jenny might be able to pick up where they left off....

"You know," Jenny murmured at that moment. "Maybe we ought to pack up and head back *before* Candy naps." When Ben opened his mouth to protest, Jenny softly added, "She might sleep all the way home...."

So Jenny preferred *packing up* to *picking up.* Well, much as he hated to admit it, she had a point. The long drive would definitely be more pleasant if Candy snoozed through most of it.

Abruptly, he got to his feet. "Let's go."

Though Ben expected the trip back home to be quiet and long, it proved to be neither. Surprisingly, he and Jenny talked like old friends.

Ben learned that she was an only child of a deceased insurance salesman and a secretary, whose second and third marriages had clearly soured Jennifer on romance and weddings.

That revelation confirmed some previous suspicions, providing much-needed insight into her psyche. And though Ben still found her bitterness confusing and somewhat daunting—convincing her otherwise would be quite a challenge, after all—it seemed to confirm that his decision to take things slow was the right one.

So what if he hadn't managed "slow" just yet? There was always next time.

What next time? he suddenly wondered, stomach knotting. Donna's arrival was mere hours away....

"How about dinner at my place before I take you home?" Ben blurted in desperation about a mile out of Springfield. "I could grill hamburgers," he added, already formulating an argument to her certain refusal.

"Why, thanks. I'd love to."

Ben gulped. *So much for slow.* Was he ready for the fast lane? he asked himself with a sidelong glance Jenny's way. His ardent gaze swept over her delicate profile then dipped to encompass every womanly inch below.

Hell, yes, he decided, at once on fire for her. He was ready for the fast lane and even for what undoubtedly lay at the end of it—marriage.

It had happened. It had really happened. Ben Ryder had fallen in love and nothing, even old goals, new fears, or those ridiculous characteristics he'd once held in high esteem—could change that.

Now all he had to do was convince Jenny—a woman he'd known mere days—to love him back.

Minutes later, a somber Ben maneuvered the truck down his rutted, dusty road. "If the weather holds, I'll be able to get this thing paved in a couple of weeks," he commented oh-so-casually as he braked a few feet from his front porch and killed the engine. "Then you won't have any trouble at all when you come over."

"I'll bet your patients will be glad."

"Not to mention their owners," Ben added with a smile.

So she wasn't averse to the idea of dropping by now and then. Good. Whistling softly, he got out and ambled around to the passenger side, where he assisted Jenny from the truck and then released his just-waked niece from the confines of her car seat. Together the three of them walked to the house.

I feel like I'm coming home, Jenny thought as she stepped into the kitchen. A traitorously warm glow began somewhere in the region of her heart and spread quickly to encompass her entire body. She marveled at it and at the woman she'd become in less than a week.

Must be love, she thought in awe. Has to be love. Nothing else could be so sweet.

As sweet as Candy? She smiled.

Who'd have thought it? And who'd have dreamed it would feel this way? No wonder her mother and Krissie had lost their heads when they lost their hearts. Love did that to a person. And the heck of it was Jenny didn't even mind anymore.

She did wonder if Ben had lost his heart, too. She hoped he had.

"Down," Candy announced, squirming to be set free.

"Not just yet," Ben told her. He turned to Jenny. "Why don't you have a seat in the den? I'm going to change Candy and then start on dinner."

"Why don't I change Candy?" Jenny asked, reaching for the child. "You can get right to work in here."

Ben laughed and handed the toddler over. "Hungry?"

"Always," Jenny told him. She turned to leave, but stopped short when Ben caught her arm.

He stood for a moment in silence looking deep into her eyes, his own promising everything she'd ever dreamed of and maybe even more. "Thanks for today," he murmured, leaning forward.

"My pleasure," she told him, just before he pressed his lips to hers.

"No, no, no." Candy immediately fussed, trying to push them apart.

"Hey! What's this?" Ben asked with a chuckle, pulling back. "Is my girl jealous? Well, she shouldn't be. I've got kisses enough for two." At that he gave his bright-eyed niece a noisy smooch on the cheek, which erased her frown and produced that magical giggle.

Smiling at their antics, Jenny shooed Ben away and walked past to the guest room in search of a disposable diaper, a once-again impatient Candy hanging over her arm like Spanish moss. When Jenny found no diapers there, she headed to Ben's bathroom where she remembered seeing a box.

Intent on her task, Jenny paid little heed to Ben's bedroom as she walked through it en route to the bath. She quickly found the diapers, stepped back into the bedroom and positioned Candy on the bed, making short work of changing her so they could go help Ben. She then picked up the toddler and moved toward the hall.

Just before Jenny stepped through the door, she spied an ornate wooden plaque hanging on the wall over Ben's desk. Intrigued by the golf tees sticking out of it, she stopped and went back for a closer look. Jenny laughed at what she saw.

"So Ben's got a list, too," she murmured. "A list of the qualities he seeks in a wife. And look... all of them have been checked off but one."

Amused, Jenny read the first two qualities aloud. "'Must have long brown hair. Must have big brown eyes.'" She stopped to consider those attributes and decided that as qualities went, these seemed reasonable enough. After all, she had both herself.

Encouraged, still smiling, Jenny dropped her gaze to item number three. "'Petite.'" Her smile faded. "Now why on earth would a man Ben's size want a woman who's petite?"

Candy didn't know or wasn't telling, and since she began to squirm with impatience, Jenny moved on to the next item. "'Must be a good cook.' Oh dear." She sighed with dismay and absently shifted her wiggling bundle to the other arm. "'Must love kids. Must be a good housekeeper....'" Now completely absorbed and downright discouraged, Jenny abruptly gave Candy her freedom and turned her full attention to the next two items. "'Must love animals. Must be a good money manager.'" She groaned aloud. "Good grief. Is he looking for a wife or a saint?"

Looking for a wife? Ben?

When? Jenny glared at the golf tees that checked off these wonderful characteristics she, herself, could never claim. It seemed that Ben had done some serious looking at one time or another, and, from all appearances, come very close to finding his Miss Right.

Except for that one, last quality.... Extremely curious, Jenny peered closer.

"'Must be good in bed.'" Jenny's face flamed. "*Good in bed!* The nerve of the man! Good in bed, indeed."

At once, Jenny wondered if that particular item wasn't checked off Ben's list because his candidate—whoever the poor soul was—had found him out.

Jenny sincerely hoped so. And she hoped Ben had learned something from the experience. The choice of one's mate should never be approached so logically. It had to be based on emotion, on love. Surely he knew that.

But of course he did. The Ben Ryder she'd come to know and cherish that week would never judge a possible partner by such a calculating, petty, chauvinistic checklist.

As for her own list...hadn't she realized *days ago* how stupid it was? Yes. And not once since then had she wondered if Ben were manipulative or preoccupied with sex, those two traits still left on it.

Pleased with herself, but a little disappointed in Ben, Jenny purposefully dismissed the plaque and turned to exit the room. Her gaze fell on a scratch pad next to Ben's phone. On it she saw her name, and scrawled under that "good in bed"...with a great big question mark after it.

Jenny's jaw dropped. She snatched up the pad and stared at it in disbelief, face flaming, heart hammering.

"Oh my God!" she exploded. "Am *I* the 'poor soul' he's rating?" Horrified, Jenny sank into Ben's chair.

He'd certainly spoken of his desire for a happy marriage, she remembered—a reasonable enough goal for a well-established, successful man of his age.

But to have these particular qualities in mind and then consider her...

Jenny laughed aloud, unable to imagine Ben's actually thinking she might make a model wife. Then she remembered her actions that week, and her laughter died.

So far she'd cooked for him, played mommy to his niece and otherwise acted like one of those female ninnies of the 1950s situation comedies. Why shouldn't Ben think she was the paragon he sought? And thinking that, why shouldn't he use Candy as an excuse to visit and call?

With a heartfelt groan, Jenny buried her face in her hands to block the sight of that hateful plaque. Then she snapped her head up again, her gaze zooming in on the last, unchecked item on Ben's list.

"Must be good in bed."

Slowly the truth hit home. Ben's kisses—Ben's wonderful, magical kisses—had probably been nothing more than an attempt to put a tee next to that quality.

To think she'd thought herself in love with the man! To think she'd wondered if he felt the same!

And to think that mere hours ago the two of them had lain side by side on a blanket in the middle of nowhere—kissing, caressing, well on their way to...

Talk about manipulative! And as for preoccupied with sex...

"Grrr!" As furious with herself as with Ben, Jenny snatched the plaque from the papered wall and stomped to the kitchen. There she found him at the counter, busy forming ground beef into patties. At his feet sat Candy, stirring air in a mixing bowl.

He looked up and smiled when she stormed into the room. "So there you are. I was beginning t-to..." Ben stuttered to a stop, his gaze on the plaque Jenny held. Slowly the color drained from his face.

"How could you?" Jenny demanded, taking his reaction as proof he was guilty as charged.

Ben dropped the meat on the counter and snatched up a dish towel to wipe his hands. "I can explain—" he began, tossing aside the towel. He took a step toward her.

Jenny stopped him with a look. "A list. *A list,* for God's sake. I can't believe it!"

"But it was just a—"

"And look at what's on it—good housekeeper, good cook, good money manager. You don't want a wife, Ben Ryder. You want a slave."

"It was a joke. My sisters—"

"I thought you were different," Jenny raged on, ignoring his attempts to explain. She shook the plaque under his nose. "I thought you were a man who could appreciate a woman for what she is, not for what she could do for you. But you're just as arrogant as all the other men in this man's world. And me...well, apparently I'm just as spineless as all the other women."

Ben snatched the plaque and slammed it onto the counter. Then he grasped Jenny's shoulders, holding her securely in front of him even when she automatically tried to break away.

"Will you just be still and listen to me? The list was a joke—*a joke,* I'm telling you. I made it to irritate the hell out of my matchmaking sisters and never, for one second, took it seriously."

"Then why are there tees in the holes?"

Ben opened his mouth to reply, then snapped it shut again. He released her, leaned against the counter and crossed his arms over his chest. "So I stuck some tees in it. So what? I'd love you even if you hadn't scored so well."

Jenny glared her outrage. Love? Had he really said love? Why, if the man loved at all—and she doubted *that*—he loved a woman who didn't really exist.

"Take me home," she demanded through clenched teeth.

He shook his head. "Not until we talk."

"We have nothing to say to each other."

"The hell we don't."

Jenny stalked to the door. "Are you going to take me home?"

"No."

"Then I'll walk."

At that, she yanked the door open and exited the kitchen, wings on her heels. Those same wings sent her flying across the porch and clear down the drive.

"You can't walk clear back to town," Ben yelled after her, clearly in a bit of a temper himself.

"Wanna bet?" Jenny muttered, stepping over an ankle-deep rut and onto the dirt road.

Behind her, the truck door slammed. A second later the engine came to life. Two seconds after that, Ben roared past and screeched to a dusty halt a few feet ahead of her.

"Get in," he ordered, leaning across his wide-eyed niece to push open the door.

Jenny never broke stride.

The truck lurched forward, then kept up with her. "Get in, Jennifer."

"You go to hell."

"Get in, dammit!"

Incensed, Jenny whirled to give Ben a piece of her mind. She took one good look at his glittering black eyes, gulped and climbed into the vehicle without another word.

Fifteen minutes and a silent ride later, she climbed back out again.

"Good night," Ben said, just as she turned to slam the door shut.

Their gazes locked. For one crazy moment, Jenny wanted to throw herself in his arms. Then sanity ruled again.

"Goodbye," she replied, silently adding, *and good riddance* as she stepped into her empty apartment.

As promised and expected, Donna and Andy Oakes stepped into Ben's house Sunday afternoon and claimed their offspring. Though Ben had longed for that moment more than once during that week, he found himself lonely and moping not ten minutes after they drove away.

Even a joyous reunion with Flicka and Beauty did not help his blue mood, and dusk found him sitting in his recliner, drumming his fingers on the armrest and listening to the dust settle.

Moments later, he leapt to his feet and paced from room to room, half expecting to stumble on to Candy, playing in a wastebasket, climbing up the dresser via the open drawers, or mutilating the plants.

That would ease his boredom, he told himself, collapsing into the recliner again. But not nearly so effectively as rounding a corner to find Jenny curled up on his couch reading his mystery, or grilling his steaks in his kitchen, or tucking in a curly-headed infant...preferably his, also.

That would never happen, of course, a truth made plain when she ignored his inadvertent declaration of love the night before. Obviously she didn't care about him nearly as much as he'd led himself to believe.

And all those kisses—those wonderful, wonderful kisses—meant nothing to her.

Ben frowned at that depressing thought, suddenly aware that the pieces of this puzzle simply didn't fit unless one of them was love. That and nothing else could explain Jenny's near hysteria over that stupid plaque, which could hurt her only if she cared.

"God, what a mess," he told his pets, who watched anxiously from their favorite, just-restored positions at his feet. "And all because of some cockamamy list I don't care beans about. What am I going to do?"

The most logical thing would be to call her and demand the truth, he decided around eight o'clock that night after four hours of staring at the walls.

But when he tried, Jenny hung up in his ear.

Fuming, Ben marched straight to his truck, got in and drove to her apartment. But she would not come to the door, and short of kicking it down—an idea that did cross his mind—Ben had no option but to go back home and think of another way to get to her.

Because get to her, he would. Later if not sooner; for now and for always.

Whether she knew it now or not, Jennifer Robbin possessed him—heart, soul and mind. And whether she wanted to now or not—she would one day be his.

Ben would settle for nothing less.

Though Jenny's temper had given her strength to resist Ben's attempts to communicate on Sunday, come Monday it dissolved into nothingness, leaving her lost, lonely and longing for him to phone or come by again.

So it was with fear—and hope—she answered her phone when it rang early that morning.

"Happy birthday to you. Happy birthday to you. Happy birthday, dear Jen-ny, happy birthday to you."

Jenny winced at the sound of Krissie, screeching the old standard. "Nice try," she murmured gloomily. "But it's no use. 'Happy' is out of the question today."

"Hmm. Sounds like thirty is hitting hard, but I have a cure—dinner at Angelo's tonight. Just picture the salad, oozing with oil and vinegar. The lasagne, smothered in sauce and cheese. The bread, smeared with butter.... Is seven too early?"

"Thanks for the invite. But I believe it would be better for all concerned if we didn't go out," Jenny replied. "I'm just not in the mood to celebrate."

"Oh, come on," Krissie responded. "Thirty isn't so bad."

"Actually, I'd forgotten it was my birthday until you reminded me," Jenny admitted. "It's well, something else."

"More like some*one* else, I'll bet," Krissie said. "Don't tell me. Let me guess. You and Ben had words."

Jenny gave a short laugh. "Don't I wish."

"What do you mean?"

"I mean the man wanted to 'have words,' but I was so darned angry I wouldn't."

"Angry? What on earth did he do?"

"You won't believe it...." Jenny began. She drew in a shaky breath, once more battling the tears of self-pity she'd held at bay the day before, then told Krissie the whole sad tale.

"You're right," her old friend announced when Jenny finished her story. "I don't believe it."

"Doesn't he have his nerve?" Jenny asked with an injured sniff, swiping at an errant tear.

"No more than you," Krissie responded.

Jenny bobbled the phone in her surprise. "What?"

"For crying out loud, Jen. You've used a list to rate your dates, for years."

"That's different."

"How?"

Jenny pondered the question for a moment then snapped, "It just is. And for your information, it's not the list that bothers me. It's the fact that Ben thinks he loves me, based on the fact that I've got all—well, almost all—the characteristics he wants in a wife, when in truth, I don't."

"So you've given your heart to a man who's given his heart to a myth."

"Exactly!" Jenny exclaimed, smiling her satisfaction that she and Krissie were finally on the same wavelength.

Krissie gave a lusty sigh. "You do realize you're basing your happiness and future on an assumption?"

"Of course I..." Jenny frowned. "What do you mean?"

"You said yourself that you wouldn't let Ben explain. What if you're wrong about his motives? What if he really loves the real you and you've tossed away the chance of a lifetime?"

"Oh, Krissie," Jenny moaned. "What am I going to do?"

"Call him?" Krissie suggested.

"I don't know. I just don't know."

"Then think on it some more and remember—a good man is hard to find."

"And you think Ben is a good man?"

"I *know* it."

"More gut instinct?" Jenny asked with a wry smile, remembering that night an eternity ago when Krissie proclaimed Ben to be stable, hardworking and established... three minutes after she met him.

"Not this time. I checked him out."

"You what?"

"I checked him out, or Jack did."

"How could you?" Jenny demanded, appalled.

"Actually it was easy. One of Jack's customers at the lumberyard, a guy named Roy something or other, called about some posts he needs to fence Ben's pasture for a horse. Jack asked him all about Ben."

"What'd he say?" The words tumbled out of Jenny's mouth.

Krissie laughed. "Exactly what I just told you. Ben is a good man. Now do yourself a big favor and give that good man a call. The way I see it, you've got nothing to lose."

"And everything to gain?"

"Exactly. So do it—and the sooner the better. You're not getting any younger, you know."

"Don't remind me," Jenny retorted with a grimace, just before she dropped the receiver back in its cradle.

Her birthday passed uneventfully, save for a bouquet of balloons from her coworkers. Jenny left those same friends with a smile and a wave that evening, nowhere nearer a decision to call Ben.

The newly awakened woman in her—the one who quivered at the memory of Ben's touch—wanted to gamble and phone him. The other woman—the one who remembered a mother's mistakes—wanted only to play it safe and get on with living.

But was life without Ben really living?

Still unsure, Jenny entered her apartment at six, just as the phone rang. Certain it was her mother, calling with birthday greetings, or maybe Krissie, calling her about dinner again, Jenny snatched up the phone. "Hello."

"Hi."

Jenny caught her breath at the sound of Ben's voice, so unexpected, so close, so sexy. *If only he were here,* she thought, the next moment thanking her lucky stars he wasn't. A telephone conversation beat the heck out of a face-to-face confrontation—at least until he gave her a clue as to how he felt about her.

"Hi, yourself."

"You're speaking to me!" Ben exclaimed, adding a rumbly laugh of pleasure. "Does that mean you're not angry anymore?"

"I did overreact," she told him, hoping that candid admission would open the door to a little honesty on his part, too.

"No, you had every right to be upset. Every right."

So far so good. "Did Donna and Andy get back all right?"

"Uh-huh. Sunday evening."

"I'll bet that big ol' house is awfully quiet."

"Quiet and lonely," he agreed. "And that's the reason I called."

Jenny's heart leapt with joy. Here it comes, she thought. The explanation that would make everything okay, followed by a real vow of love, followed by... a proposal. She could barely breathe. "Is that so?"

"Yeah. I was so miserable tonight that I called Donna and volunteered to baby-sit while she and Andy celebrated their anniversary."

"Oh..."

"Unfortunately, Candy is wild as a March hare and Donna and Andy aren't due back for hours."

"Oh."

"She says she wants you, so I thought I'd call and—"

Jenny didn't wait to hear any more. Disappointed, angry all over again, she depressed the switchhook, cutting him off midsentence. When certain she'd broken the connection, she quickly dialed Krissie's number.

"Hello?"

"May I change my mind about dinner tonight?" Jenny asked.

"Of course," Krissie told her, with obvious curiosity adding, "Why?"

"Because I've got better things to do than spend my birthday mooning over a selfish, spoiled, manipulative, arrogant jerk who is definitely, but definitely, preoccupied with sex!"

Chapter Ten

Jenny glanced around her, trying to absorb the serenity of Angelo's, her favorite Italian restaurant. Two hours had passed since she hung up on Ben—two hours spent washing her hair, fixing her face, slipping into her best dress and wondering if she'd miss those things when doing time for murder.

She decided that a lifetime behind bars—even without lipstick—would be well worth the pleasure of wringing Ben's neck. Now all she had to do was catch him alone....

"Eat your dinner," Krissie said, breaking into her plans.

"Yes, Mother," Jenny retorted. She picked up a fork, took a bite of her salad and chewed without tasting, oblivious to the perfectly set table, the snowy linen cloth and the flickering tapers, which usually gave her so much pleasure.

"Good, huh?"

"Could you please pick another adjective?" Jenny asked with a grimace, tossing down her fork. "I'm a little down on 'good' at the moment."

Krissie sighed and lay down her own fork. "I'm so sorry things turned out like this. What a way to spend your birthday... and I wanted everything to be so nice."

Jenny suddenly took note of her friend's down-turned mouth and misty eyes. At once remorseful for spoiling Krissie's evening, she mustered a smile from somewhere and reached out to pat her hand. "Hey, cheer up. Maybe it isn't so bad."

Krissie frowned at her. "How can you say that? You just got dumped, for crying out loud."

"It's simply a matter of putting things in perspective. So what if I don't have a man in my life? I have other, more important things."

"Name one."

"I'll name more than one. I'm thirty years old, educated, solvent. I have a nice apartment, good friends and an active social calendar."

Krissie arched an eyebrow at that, but said nothing.

"I'm wholehearted—"

"Wholehearted?"

"Wholehearted. I'm footloose. I'm fancy-free. *And* I have a wonderful, upwardly mobile career. What more could a woman ask for?"

"I knew it!" Krissie groaned. "I told Jack you'd probably apply for that job in Kansas City now and you've gone and done it, haven't you?"

Job in...? Jenny almost laughed at the mention of that directorship she'd once thought so intriguing. It hadn't crossed her mind in days and now that she thought about it, she wasn't at all sure it interested her anymore.

"Not yet," she nonetheless replied thoughtfully. "But I can't think of a single reason why I shouldn't."

"I can," Krissie retorted. "Her name starts with a *K* and ends with an *r-i-s-s-i-e*. You cannot move to Kansas City. I'll just die without you."

"You have Jack, you ninny," Jenny replied. "I'm the one who's going to be alone."

"No thanks to Ben Ryder," Krissie grumbled, a sentiment that brought a tender smile to Jenny's lips. Trust Krissie to be on her side when the chips were down. "Some *good man* he turned out to be."

"Hey, now. I probably won't apply for that job, and if I do, I probably won't be selec—" Jenny broke off, noting that the eyes of her loyal friend had suddenly widened in obvious shock. Turning, she sought the source of that shock, and then gasped her own.

"Isn't that Candy?" Krissie whispered as the waiter led a man, woman and child past their table en route to another.

"It sure is, and she's with her parents. Ben must have given up and called them. That's too bad...." Jenny watched in silence until Andy and Donna were seated at a table a few feet away, Candy between them in a high chair. As though sensing the intensity of Jenny's gaze, Donna suddenly glanced up, smiled and waved—a friendly gesture Jenny found encouraging.

Impulsively, she got to her feet and walked over to their table. "Happy anniversary."

Andy, a look of sheer panic on his face, glanced uncertainly at his pretty wife. "Did I forget our anniversary?"

"Not unless this is *June* twentieth," Donna told him with a laugh, reaching out to pat his suddenly flushed cheek. Obviously not convinced, Andy looked down at his watch, as though to verify that the date block on it said September twentieth. Donna laughed again.

"You mean it's not your anniversary?" Jenny asked, frowning.

"I'm afraid not," Donna replied.

"But Ben said..." Jenny shook her head and shrugged. "I must have misunderstood him when he called and asked me to come help him with Candy tonight."

"He asked you to...?" Donna exchanged a puzzled look with her blue-eyed, blond-haired husband. "Now why would Ben ask Jenny for help tonight? I told him we were going to get a family picture made and then eat out."

"Maybe he's thinking about Thursday," Andy replied. He gave Jenny a smile. "We bowl in a pairs tournament that night."

"Must be Thursday," Donna agreed.

"But Ben told me Candy was there already," Jenny responded. "He said he couldn't handle her and asked me to come over—" She broke off, suddenly flustered as a possible, too-good-to-be-true reason for his lie came to mind. Could it be that Ben had been using his niece as an excuse to call all week?

Donna exchanged another long look with her handsome husband, this one amused... and very embarrassing to Jenny. "I take it you refused."

"Actually I hung up on him," Jenny admitted.

Donna bubbled with laughter at that. "Serves that brother of mine right for lying. I knew he was dying to see you again, but I had no idea he was that desperate."

Jenny's heart leapt. "Desperate?"

"As in ready to club you over the head and drag you off to a cave somewhere," Andy put in. He shook his own head slowly from side to side. "And to think Ben used to be one of the kindest, most gentle men I know. It's pitiful what love can do to a guy."

"Shhh," Donna warned. "You're speaking out of turn."

"It's time somebody did," Andy retorted. He looked Jenny dead in the eye and shook a finger at her. "I realize that what you and Ben do is none of my business—"

"So hush," Donna interjected in an obvious attempt to quiet him.

"But I'm still going to have my say," Andy continued, ignoring her. "If you love that man, for God's sake tell him, because he's sure in love with you."

With me? Or with a fantasy woman? Jenny asked herself seconds later as she snatched up her purse, mumbled an explanation and left a thrilled and ever-hopeful Krissie on the phone, cajoling her husband into abandoning his football game to join her for a dinner á deux.

Jenny drove straight to Ben's house, both hands clutching the steering wheel so she could maneuver the potholes in his road. The dark of night and her high speed did not help one bit, and by the time Jenny halted her car, she trembled with agitation.

She sat there long moments, staring at his door, trying to get up the nerve to follow through on her impulse. What if Andy was wrong? she agonized. What if Ben wasn't in love with her at all?

Then this is your chance to do him in, she told herself with a nervous giggle, reaching for the door handle. After taking in a couple of deep, calming breaths, Jenny swallowed back the second thoughts that seemed to have lumped in her throat, and walked with new determination to the porch. A second later, she knocked loudly on the kitchen door.

Ben's silhouette darkened the filmy curtain covering the small, head-high window almost immediately, a sure sign he'd heard her noisy approach and maybe even looked out to see who'd come to call. Jenny saw him finger-comb his hair and straighten the collar of his shirt, little moves that warmed her heart and made her glad she'd swallowed her pride and taken a gamble.

I'll just be honest with him, she told herself. I'll explain who and what I really am—a less-than-perfect woman who's wild about him—and maybe, just maybe it'll be enough for a new start.

God, but she hoped so. She could not comprehend a lifetime without his kiss.

At that moment, the door opened and Ben stood before her. He smiled slightly in greeting, but said nothing, his warm gaze caressing her from freshly curled hair to shimmery blue dress to matching pumps. Jenny's temperature shot up several degrees when his glowing eyes finally met hers again.

Never had she felt so cherished, so vibrantly alive, so tempted to swear she was the woman he wanted.

But that would be a lie...and it was time he found out.

"We need to talk," she said instead. "May I come in?"

Without a word, Ben stepped aside and motioned her into the kitchen. At once he led the way to the den, where they both sat rather stiffly on opposite ends of the couch.

"Why did you call and tell me you were baby-sitting Candy tonight?" Jenny asked, getting straight to the point.

He didn't seem surprised by the question and he didn't try to deny his lie. "I didn't think you'd see me otherwise, and I've got to explain about the other night—about this whole week, in fact."

Jenny pondered his words for a moment before settling back on the cushions. She crossed her legs at the knee and her arms over her chest. "You have the floor."

Ben got to his feet immediately and began to pace the room, his brows knitted in a frown, his fingertips stuffed into the back pockets of his acid-washed jeans.

Lord, what a sight, Jenny thought, ready to do a little clubbing and dragging of her own. There were definitely merits to a make-love-now, talk-later-if-you-still-need-to scenario.

Suddenly Ben stopped right in front of her. "I don't know where to begin," he admitted.

"Begin with the plaque," Jenny replied. "Did you really make up that awful list?"

Ben winced. "I made it up," he said, dropping down on the couch, too close for comfort. "But only to get four sisters off my case." He shrugged. "They kept bringing over this and that possible, trying to marry me off.... I got so damn sick of it that I made the list and said if they found a woman who had all those traits, they could bring her over. Otherwise, I wanted them to butt out."

At once sympathetic and wondering if Krissie might have taken lessons from one of Ben's sisters, Jenny almost laughed. "So the list really was a joke?"

"Hell, yeah, it was a joke," Ben said.

"Then why did you put tees in the holes? And why did you write my name on that piece of paper right above 'good in bed'?"

"I never did that," Ben exclaimed, clearly outraged.

"Oh, yes you did," Jenny retorted. "I'll show you." She got to her feet and headed for the bedroom, Ben at her heels. "See?" she said, snatching up the scratch pad in question.

Ben took a good look at it and blanched. "I swear I don't remember doing that."

"But it's your handwriting?" Jenny persisted, determined to get to the bottom of things.

"Yeah..."

"I thought so, and that proves that at some point you were wondering about my sexual prowess."

Ben heaved a sigh of impatience. "If I had your sexual prowess on my mind, it was only because I wanted to be on the receiving end of it, not because I intended to give you a grade on performance. The truth is, I love you, Jenny, and always will—a fact which has nothing whatsoever to do with my asinine list."

There they were. The words for which she longed. Jenny's heart leapt with joy.

"You say that," she said, fighting to keep her excitement from her voice. "But are you really sure you mean what you say?" She reached to retrieve the wooden plaque, laying on his desk near the scratch pad, tees intact. Then motioned for Ben to sit on the bed. "I'm not the woman you think I am, Ben Ryder."

"You're woman enough for me," he said.

Ignoring that heartwarming reply with difficulty, Jenny perched on the edge of the desk and held up the plaque so Ben could see it. Deliberately, she skipped over the first two items to pull the tee out of the hole next to "petite."

"I'm not, you know," she said.

"I don't know what I was thinking of when I put that on there," he replied. "Actually, I prefer tall and slender."

Jenny nodded solemnly, then removed the tee next to "Must be a good cook." "You may as well know I hate to cook. And if I don't have a TV dinner in the freezer, I eat out." She raised her gaze to his. "Do you still say you love me?"

"I say I love you," he told her, a hint of a smile lifting the corners of his mouth. "And I also say 'what the hell?'" he added, his smile now a bit cocky. "I'm a great cook."

Jenny dragged her gaze away from those gleaming white teeth with effort and skipped over the tee beside "Must love kids," a tee she did deserve, to one she definitely did not—"Must be a good housekeeper."

"I never dust. I never mop. I never vacuum. I never make up a bed. In other words, I'm a total slob."

"But your apartment was spotless," Ben pointed out.

"I have a housekeeper. She comes in once a week." Again her gaze met his. "Do you still say you love me?"

Ben grinned, clearly not in the least perturbed by that revelation. "More than ever."

Jenny savored that for a moment, then passed over "Must love animals" to "Must be a good money manager," a tee she extracted with a vengeance. "I hate posting books and only do it because it's part of my job. An accountant does the real book work. Worse, I can't even balance my own checkbook. Do you still say you love me?"

"Yes, yes, yes, I say it," Ben declared, reaching out for her. "And I mean it, too." Though Jenny sincerely believed his words and desperately wanted that hug, she held him at bay.

"Now about this last item," she murmured, pointing to "Must be good in bed." "To be honest, I really don't know if a tee should be put there or not. I'm rather inexperienced in that department...."

"I'll be more than glad to do some research," Ben promised, at long last tugging her into his loving embrace.

"That had better be a proposal," Jenny told him as she wrapped her arms around his waist. "I'm so crazy in love that I just might let you."

Though Ben said nothing, his bone-crushing hug spoke volumes, and long moments passed before he dipped his head and gave her the kiss she craved.

Long and thorough, the kiss demonstrated quite clearly that Ben was crazy in love, too... and with none other than the woman in his arms.

It was much later, after they'd popped corn and watched *The Hound of the Baskervilles,* that Jenny raised her head from Ben's shoulder, and looked deep into his eyes. Relishing the tight squeeze of the corduroy recliner they shared, Jenny snuggled closer still and slipped her fingers between two of the buttons on his striped cotton shirt.

"Ben?" she murmured, lightly raking her nails across the bare flesh she discovered there. The muscles jumped in response.

"Hmm?"

"How many children do you want?"

He never even hesitated. "Oh, seven or eight should be about right."

"Good grief!" Jenny exclaimed, raising her head again. "I'm thirty years old. If I have eight kids, I'll still be changing diapers when I start drawing my retirement. Would you settle for one or two, instead?"

He laughed and pushed her head back down on his shoulder. "You're thirty?"

She sighed with regret. "As of today."

"It's your birthday?"

"Yes," she admitted, rather gloomily.

"Happy birthday, Jenny Wren," Ben exclaimed, punctuating the wish with a kiss. "Why don't we slip down the hall, slip out of these clothes and slip between the sheets for a private celebration?"

Jenny smiled with anticipation at the picture his words painted. "First answer my question."

He sighed. "Since I'm thirty-nine, myself, one or two kids seems perfectly reasonable and a lot more practical. I do have one request, though."

"And what's that?" she asked.

"Let's wait a while before we make those babies. Having just spent a week with Candy, I now know how disrupting a little one can be. And, frankly, celibacy would be damned rough now that I've finally found the woman of my dreams."

Jenny laughed, well remembering all the times Candy had disturbed them. "Sounds fine to me. I want some uninterrupted time with you, too."

"Starting tonight?" Ben asked with a hopeful glance toward the bedroom.

"Starting tonight," she assured him, a reply lost in the ringing of the telephone.

Ben eyed the phone, but made no move to answer it.

"Aren't you going to get that?" Jenny asked.

He shook his head and got to his feet, tugging her to hers.

"But what if it's a patient?" she protested as he nudged her in the direction of the bedroom.

"They can tell their problems to the answering ma—aw hell! It isn't even on." Muttering under his breath, Ben jogged the remaining distance to his bedroom and snatched the telephone up to his ear. "Hello." His eyebrows shot up in disbelief. "Candy? *Is that you?*"

Jenny followed and collapsed onto his bed, somehow holding her threatening laughter in check while Ben "talked" to his niece and then his sister, who, from the sound of things, simply couldn't stand the suspense any longer. The moment Ben hung up the phone and met Jenny's gaze, a look of utter disgust on his face, she gave in to her mirth.

"This isn't funny," he scolded. But she spotted the smile teasing the corners of his mouth.

"Sorry," Jenny murmured, swiping at a tear. "Now where were we?"

"I think we'd just agreed that some uninterrupted time together would be very nice—and quite a novelty, I might add."

Jenny patted the mattress beside her. When Ben sat down, she framed his face with her hands. "Something tells me that whether we have one baby or a houseful, we'll always find time for each other."

"Where there's a will, there's a way?" Ben teased with a sexy chuckle, pulling her close.

Jenny returned the hug. "Exactly," she replied. "And, believe me, I have the will."

"So do I," Ben said, even as he eased out of her loving embrace to flick a switch on the nearby answering machine. "And *this,* Jenny Wren, is the way."

Epilogue

Ben locked the door of his clinic and glanced toward his house, where bright lights glowed. He smiled with pleasure at the sight and walked through the dark with quickened steps, eager as always to be with Jenny, his wife of thirteen months.

He shook his head, marveling at how quickly the time had passed since they'd exchanged wedding vows in a private ceremony. They'd learned so much about each other, and had a ball doing so. More secure than ever in their love, they now awaited the birth of their firstborn. Suddenly anxious to know the results of the ultrasound Jenny had undergone that day, Ben bounded onto the deck and into the den. There he found his beloved wife, sitting on the couch with her feet propped up, just as she'd promised.

Though she smiled and stretched lazily, Ben wasn't fooled for a moment. Most likely she'd just that minute lain down, and only then because he'd sworn he would be home by nine for sure. Even with her tummy rounded over six months' worth of unborn baby, Jenny Ryder possessed an amazing amount of energy and even more stubbornness.

"Hi," she told him, standing up and stepping around his dog and cat to receive the hug and kiss he had waiting for her. "How's the patient?"

"Actually the patient's doing a lot better than his master," Ben replied with a grin, remembering the chaos of the past three hours spent patching up a feisty tom who'd lost a fight. "I thought I was going to have to give Clarence the anesthetic instead of Rover."

"Clarence's cat is named *Rover?*"

"Uh-huh. Isn't that clever?"

"Only to a man with a cat named Flicka and a dog named Beauty," Jenny told him, stooping to pet said cat and dog. She then straightened up with a groan.

"You okay?" Ben asked with a worried frown.

"Fine," she assured him. "Just twenty pounds heavier and feeling it right here." She put a hand to the small of her back.

"Want me to rub it for you?"

"Sounds heavenly," Jenny replied. "But first I want to show you the ultrasound."

"Everything was all right...?" Ben asked, even as she pushed him in the direction of the couch.

"Everything was perfect." Jenny sat beside him and reached for the remote control. In seconds, the television screen flickered with the image of their unborn child.

Ben's eyes misted at the precious sight. Awed by this miracle of life, created by their love, he pulled his wife close. Unashamed, he swiped at a tear while he watched their baby stretch and turn, a move which revealed another, identical shape behind it.

"Holy moly!" he exclaimed, sitting bolt upright. "Is that... ? Are we... ?"

Positively beaming, Jenny nodded. "Twins."

"But how... ?"

"You know very well how," she teased. "Too well, in fact."

Ben, ready to explode with joy and pride, laughed aloud. "Hey, now, don't blame me. This never would have happened if you hadn't been so good in bed."

Jenny just smiled in response, silently adding that it didn't hurt to have a husband who was "preoccupied with sex."

* * * * *

Love has a language all its own, and for centuries, flowers have symbolized love's finest expression. Discover the language of flowers—and love—in this romantic collection of 48 favorite books by bestselling author Nora Roberts.

Starting in February, two titles will be available each month at your favorite retail outlet.

In March, look for:

Irish Rose, **Volume #3**
Storm Warning, **Volume #4**

In April, look for:

First Impressions, **Volume #5**
Reflections, **Volume #6**

Collect all 48 titles and become fluent in

THE LANGUAGE of LOVE

Silhouette®

LOL392

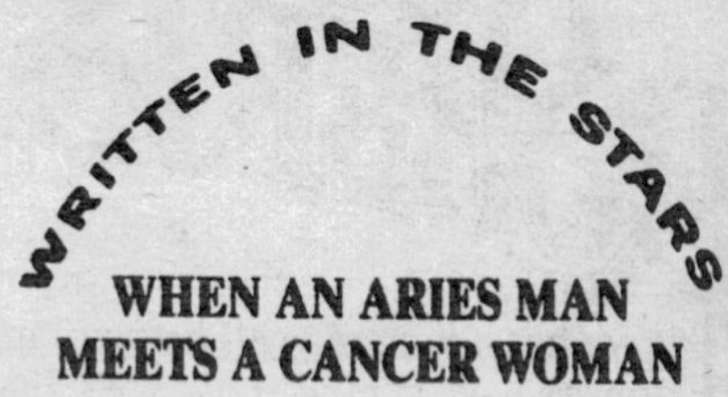

WHEN AN ARIES MAN MEETS A CANCER WOMAN

Aggressive Aries businessman Alexander Donaldson III did *not* appreciate being wakened at dawn by a huge sheep outside his bedroom window! But upon confronting its owner—child psychologist Hannah Martinof—Alex knew his love phobia was instantly cured! Now, if only Hannah would admit she wanted *him!* Carla Cassidy's WHATEVER ALEX WANTS . . . is coming this April—only from Silhouette Romance. It's WRITTEN IN THE STARS!

Available in April at your favorite retail outlet, or order your copy now by sending your name, address, zip or postal code, along with a check or money order for $2.69 (please do not send cash), plus 75¢ postage and handling ($1.00 in Canada), payable to Silhouette Reader Service to:

In the U.S.
3010 Walden Ave.
P.O. Box 1396
Buffalo, NY 14269-1396

In Canada
P.O. Box 609
Fort Erie, Ontario
L2A 5X3

Please specify book title with your order.
Canadian residents add applicable federal and provincial taxes.

SR492

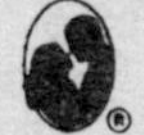

Silhouette Romance®

Silhouette Special Edition®

is pleased to present

A GOOD MAN WALKS IN
by Ginna Gray

The story of one strong woman's comeback
and the man who was there for her, Travis McCall,
the renegade cousin to those Blaine siblings,
from Ginna Gray's bestselling trio

FOOLS RUSH IN (#416)
WHERE ANGELS FEAR (#468)
ONCE IN A LIFETIME (#661)

Rebecca Quinn sought shelter at the hideaway on Rincon Island. Finding Travis McCall—the object of all her childhood crushes—holed up in the same house threatened to ruin the respite she so desperately needed. Until their first kiss... Then Travis set out to prove to his lovely Rebecca that man can be good and love, sublime.

You'll want to be there when Rebecca's disillusionment turns to joy.

A GOOD MAN WALKS IN #722

Available at your favorite retail outlet this February.

SEGG

From the popular author of the bestselling title DUNCAN'S BRIDE (Intimate Moments #349) comes the

LINDA HOWARD COLLECTION

Two exquisite collector's editions that contain four of Linda Howard's early passionate love stories. To add these special volumes to your own library, be sure to look for:

VOLUME ONE: *Midnight Rainbow*
Diamond Bay
(Available in March)

VOLUME TWO: *Heartbreaker*
White Lies
(Available in April)

SLH92